HARLEQUIN®
Presents~

Welcome to a month of fantastic reading, brought to you by Harlequin Presents! Continuing our magnificent series THE ROYAL HOUSE OF NIROLI is Melanie Milburne with *Surgeon Prince, Ordinary Wife*. With the first heir excluded from the throne of Niroli, missing prince and brilliant surgeon Dr. Alex Hunter is torn between duty and his passion for a woman who can never be his queen.... Don't miss out!

Also for your reading pleasure is the first book of Sandra Marton's new THE BILLIONAIRES' BRIDES trilogy, *The Italian Prince's Pregnant Bride*, where Prince Nicolo Barbieri acquires Aimee Black, who, it seems, is pregnant with Nicolo's baby! Then favorite author Lynne Graham brings you a gorgeous Greek in *The Petrakos Bride*, where Maddie comes face-to-face again with her tycoon idol....

In *His Private Mistress* by Chantelle Shaw, Italian racing driver Rafael is determined to make Eden his mistress once more...while in *One-Night Baby* by Susan Stephens, another Italian knows nothing of the secret Kate is hiding from their one night together. If a sheikh is what gets your heart thumping, Annie West brings you *For the Sheikh's Pleasure*, where Sheikh Arik is determined to get Rosalie to open up to receive the loving that only *he* can give her! In *The Brazilian's Blackmail Bargain* by Abby Green, Caleb makes Maggie an offer she just can't refuse. And finally Lindsay Armstrong's *The Rich Man's Virgin* tells the story of a fiercely independent woman who finds she's pregnant by a powerful millionaire. Look out for more brilliant books next month!

MISTRESS TO A MILLIONAIRE

*She's his in the bedroom,
but he can't buy her love...*

Showered with diamonds, draped in
exquisite lingerie, whisked around the world
in the lap of luxury...

The ultimate fantasy becomes a reality.

Live the dream with more
MISTRESS TO A MILLIONAIRE
titles by your favorite authors.

Available only in Harlequin Presents®

Chantelle Shaw

HIS PRIVATE MISTRESS

MISTRESS
TO A
MILLIONAIRE

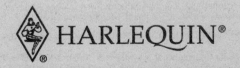

HARLEQUIN®

TORONTO • NEW YORK • LONDON
AMSTERDAM • PARIS • SYDNEY • HAMBURG
STOCKHOLM • ATHENS • TOKYO • MILAN • MADRID
PRAGUE • WARSAW • BUDAPEST • AUCKLAND

ISBN-13: 978-0-373-12654-5
ISBN-10: 0-373-12654-9

HIS PRIVATE MISTRESS

First North American Publication 2007.

All about the author...
Chantelle Shaw

CHANTELLE SHAW lives on the Kent coast, five minutes from the sea, and does much of her thinking about the characters in her books while walking on the beach. An avid reader from an early age, she found that school friends used to hide their books when she visited, but Chantelle would retreat into her own world, and she still writes stories in her head all the time.

Chantelle has been blissfully married to her own tall, dark and very patient hero for over twenty years and has six children. She began to read Harlequin novels as a teenager, and throughout the years of being a stay-at-home mom to her brood, she found romance fiction helped her to stay sane! Her aim is to write books that provide an element of escapism, fun and of course romance for the countless women who juggle work and a home life and who need their precious moments of "me" time. She enjoys reading and writing about strong-willed, feisty women and even stronger-willed sexy heroes.

Chantelle is at her happiest when writing. She is particularly inspired while cooking dinner, which unfortunately results in a lot of culinary disasters! She also loves gardening, taking her very badly behaved terrier for walks and eating chocolate (followed by more walking—at least the dog is slim!).

CHAPTER ONE

'…AND IN A round-up of local news, staff and patients at Greenacres, the specialist spinal injury unit here in Wellworth, had an unexpected visitor yesterday. Formula 1 champion Rafael Santini arrived by helicopter and spent several hours chatting to everyone at the unit before making a substantial donation. Greenacres manager, Jean Collins, said everyone was excited by the visit,' the radio presenter chuckled. 'I bet the ladies were excited, Santini's reputation off the track is as legendary as on it, if you know what I mean! Before you tell us what the weather has in store, Kate, what do you think of Rafe Santini?'

'Oh, a sex god, definitely, Brian. He'd brighten my day, which is more than can be said for the forecast…'

Eden stabbed her finger on the radio control button, cutting off the presenter's irritatingly bright voice, and stared impatiently at the queue of traffic. The roadworks had sprung up as if by magic overnight and she drummed her fingers on the wheel, refusing to admit that her tension had more to do with nerves than the fact that she was late. She shouldn't have had that second glass of wine last night, she conceded when she finally reached the hotel. No doubt it was the reason she had overslept and was responsible for the dull ache across her temples.

Her high heels clicked on the marble tiles of the foyer and a hasty glance in the mirror revealed that she looked cool and elegant in her cream trouser suit, her long blonde hair falling in a thick braid down her back. Her air of composure disguised the fact that her heart was racing. There was no good reason for the sick feeling in the pit of her stomach, she berated herself; it was ridiculous to feel so *nervous*.

Security at the front desk was tight; she should have expected it, and her irritation grew as she scrabbled in her bag for her Press pass, barely able to contain her impatience as the security guard scrutinised it carefully before waving her through. It would be easier to break into Fort Knox, she decided grimly when she was stopped at the door to the conference hall by another security guard.

'You are late,' the guard informed her unnecessarily, in his slow, carefully pronounced English. 'The interview has already begun.'

'I'll slip in quietly,' Eden promised. 'No one will notice.' She prayed she was right; the last thing she wanted to do was draw attention to herself. If the morning had gone to plan she would already be safely ensconced at the back of the room, buried amidst the huddle of other journalists, unnoticed and anonymous.

The conference hall was packed and again she wondered what she had expected. Rafael Santini rarely gave interviews. He had a love-hate relationship with the media, whereby they loved to report his every move and he abhorred their intrusion into his private life. Since his brother Gianni's terrible accident three years ago, and the fevered media speculation that Rafe had been responsible for the crash, his feelings for the paparazzi had developed into an almost pathological hatred. Even now, in his exalted position as Formula 1 World Champion, his statements to the Press had been condensed into a few terse words and Eden wondered what form of persuasion Fabrizzio Santini had used to coerce his eldest son to face the media.

Eden kept her head lowered as she slunk into one of the last empty seats at the back of the hall, and it was only then, when she was well and truly hidden, that she dared to lift her eyes to the stage. She had been mentally preparing for this moment all morning. Hell, who was she kidding? She had been on edge for days, ever since she had known that she was going to see Rafe again. Even so, that first sight of him, the sheer impact of his stunningly handsome face, caused her to inhale sharply, her stomach churning, and she dropped her gaze, needing to reassemble her defences.

Rafael Santini looked bored. His hard features were schooled into a mask of polite interest, the chiselled perfection of his bone structure, the aquiline nose and heavy black brows from beneath which gleamed eyes the colour of polished jet, acting as a magnet for every woman in the room. But even from a distance Eden could read the signs of his impatience. It was there in the rigid set of his jaw, the way he twiddled a pen between his fingers, his smile revealing a flash of white teeth, but not reaching his eyes. As she watched him he stiffened, his body suddenly taut, his dark eyes hooded as he stared across the room in her direction. He couldn't possibly know she was there, Eden reassured herself as she sank lower in her seat. Rafe knew she was a journalist and that she came from Wellworth; it was where they had first met, after all. Doubtless he would also assume that she retained her links with the spinal-injury unit that he had just presented with a generous donation, but he would not expect her to be at the Press conference, and the air of tension that emanated from him was just a trick of her imagination.

Hadn't he always been aware of her the moment she entered a room? the voice in her head insidiously reminded her. It was a sixth sense they had shared, their consciousness of each other so acute that even in a crowded room they had known the exact moment the other was near. It was a memory long buried and she wished it hadn't surfaced now. She preferred to remember Rafe as a distant, unemotional lover who had provided great sex but little else. That was one of the reasons she had decided to end their relationship, if he hadn't beaten her to it and dumped her so publicly. It was surprising how much it hurt, even after all this time, and the sudden, stark memory of just how emotional their relationship had been was an unwelcome intrusion into her well-ordered life.

A woman at the front of the hall asked Rafe to speculate on his chances of winning Silverstone in two days' time and he relaxed slightly, his sexy smile causing a cramping pain in the pit of Eden's stomach.

'I don't speculate,' he answered with the careless arrogance she remembered so well. 'I intend to win. The car is performing well, and so am I,' he murmured throatily, with a suggestive wink at the young journalist, who visibly wilted under the force of his charm. A ripple of laughter ran through the crowd at his answer. He wasn't known as the Italian Stallion for nothing—stories of his numerous affairs hit the headlines on a regular basis—and Eden gritted her teeth as she reached for her notebook.

A few basic details, information gleaned from questions she would leave the other journalists to ask. Cliff couldn't expect any more, and if he did he was going to be disappointed because no way was she going to try and snatch an exclusive interview with Rafe Santini. Once, she might have been overwhelmed by his seductive Latin charm, like the young journalist who was still looking flushed and starry-eyed, but she was no longer the impressionable girl who had fallen in love with the world's number-one Lothario.

She knew that her old friend, Cliff Harley, the editor of the *Wellworth Gazette*, was hoping for an in-depth account of the life of Formula 1's ultimate hero.

'Come on, Eden, you're the golden girl, the hotshot reporter, renowned for her daring escapades in Africa,' he had cajoled. 'If anyone can get a good story from the Santini racing team Press interview, it's you.'

'Rafe Santini loathes the media,' Eden argued, 'and he's almost certainly not going to grant any exclusive interviews. I imagine he's only agreed to the Press conference to promote the fact that the Santini group have bought out the sports-car manufacturers in Oxford. It's a damage-limitation exercise after the scandals that have hit the Santini team over the last few years.'

'Yeah, but you have the added bonus of knowing Rafe intimately,' Cliff teased with a salacious grin, and Eden blushed. Oh, yes, she had known Rafe intimately, had been so familiar with every inch of his body that even now, four years on, she could picture his broad, olive-skinned chest, the muscled hardness of his thighs and his powerful physique.

'My friendship with Rafe ended a long time ago,' she told Cliff primly, ignoring his smirk at her description of Rafe as her friend. To be fair, Cliff was right; she had never been Rafael Santini's friend. His mistress, yes, his sexual playmate, whom he had picked up and cast aside whenever he felt like it and whom he had seemed to delight in flaunting before the public as his besotted lover, yes. But the intimacy they shared had never run any deeper than that.

'Well, I want a story with a bit of depth,' Cliff told her. 'I want details, I want to know what makes Santini tick, how he feels just before a race. I want a story that exposes the man behind the myth...'

'You want to know who he's sleeping with,' Eden muttered caustically, cutting Cliff off in mid-flow. Five years ago they'd started out together as junior reporters on the *Gazette*, but since then their lives had taken very different paths. Cliff had remained in Wellworth, married his childhood sweetheart and worked his way up to editor, while she had earned a reputation as a fearless and respected foreign correspondent sending back reports from the trouble-torn Ivory Coast. She'd spent the last three years living on her wits and she needed a break, time to recover.

She had promised her parents she would do nothing more energetic than sit in the garden of their cottage, but after a month of inactivity she was climbing the walls and was grateful for Cliff's offer of a job as a reporter for the *Gazette*. 'I won't do sleaze,' she had warned as she headed out of the office. 'One of the lessons I learned from the year I spent with Rafe was what it feels like to have your face plastered across the tabloids and a load of rubbish written about you.'

Frantically, she shut off the unpleasant memories and scribbled down a few more notes about Rafe's intention to continue competing in Formula 1 for the foreseeable future. There had been talk that Fabrizzio Santini was not in the best of health and certainly he had been devastated by the accident that had left his younger son, Gianni, paralysed. It was rumoured that Fabrizzio wanted to hand over the reins of the Santini Corporation to Rafael, but Eden hadn't taken them seriously. Rafe would never give up racing; it was in his blood, the need for speed and excitement, a degree of competitiveness that had put him at the head of his sport for a decade.

Rafe wasn't like other men. There was a wild element to him that saw him take risks that others would have regarded as madness, but which he always managed to pull off successfully. Many aspired to be like him, not least his younger brother, Gianni, but the rivalry between them had grown beyond the bounds of sibling competitiveness and had ultimately led to Gianni's terrible crash.

It was warm in the conference hall and the journalist sitting next to Eden was overweight and sweating profusely as he juggled with his notebook and a plastic beaker of coffee. He dropped his pen and as he leant forwards to retrieve it he sent a stream of scalding liquid into her lap.

'Oh, heck—sorry, love,' he muttered as Eden yelped and half stood, frantically trying to blot the spreading stain with a tissue.

'Yes, the young lady in the corner.' Rafe's agent's voice sounded from the stage, followed by a long silence.

'He means you,' another reporter hissed to Eden and she flushed and quickly sat down.

'I don't have a question,' she muttered, and the reporter sighed impatiently.

'Well, think of one, for Christ's sake, before Santini gets fed up and ends the interview. He's not known for his patience.'

Aware that her continuing silence was attracting curious glances, she took a deep breath. She had no option but to say something, she realised dismally, but her mind had gone blank and she asked the first question that came into her head. 'Mr Santini, does your interest and financial support for the spinal unit in Wellworth stem from the injuries your brother received in his accident at the Hungarian Grand Prix?'

A murmur rustled through the crowd of journalists, more heads turned in her direction and Eden slid lower into her seat, praying that she had disguised her voice sufficiently that Rafe wouldn't recognise her. It was four years, she reminded herself; with any luck he would give a brief answer and move on.

'You've done it now,' the reporter standing close to her groaned. 'Didn't you hear Santini's agent say at the beginning of the Press call that Rafe won't tolerate any questions about his personal life and, in particular, anything about his brother?'

'I came in late,' Eden said, trying to defend herself. 'I didn't know.'

Up on the stage Rafe had leaned towards his companion and the two men were involved in a heated discussion before his agent stared in Eden's direction. 'Mr Santini requests that you repeat the question, but first will you please stand and state your name?'

So much for remaining anonymous, Eden thought grimly as she eyed the side-exit and debated making an escape bid. It was too late; all eyes were on her and she had no choice but to slowly stand up. Even then she clung to the faint hope that he would not recognise her across the distance of the conference hall, but as she glanced towards the stage the room seemed to miraculously empty and there was no one but Rafe.

Dark eyes studied her with insolent appraisal, stripped her layer by layer and left her bare and exposed. She felt as though he had bored into her and captured her soul, and then suddenly his eyes released her from their hold and she shivered at the level of contempt in his gaze.

'Eden Lawrence from the *Wellworth Gazette*,' she said huskily, forcing the words past the lump in her throat. There was no point in lying about her identity now that he had recognised her. 'I wondered if Mr Santini's patronage of Greenacres, the centre that specialises in aiding those with spinal injuries, was because of the accident that left his brother paralysed?' Her head was thumping; she felt her cheeks burn and gripped the back of a chair as she was subjected to another cold, hard stare.

'Mr Santini wishes to point out that he makes donations to many charitable organisations,' Rafe's agent snapped, 'but, as was made clear at the beginning of this interview, he will not answer any questions regarding his personal life.'

Suitably chastened, Eden went to sit down, but was halted by a voice that even now, with the distance of years to protect her, sent a shiver of awareness down her spine.

'Miss Lawrence, I am flattered by your fascination with my private life, and it's true that there are very…personal reasons for my support of the spinal-injury unit, which does such excellent work.'

There was no evading Rafe's gaze, however hard she tried. Her eyes seemed to be drawn to him by a magnetic pull so that she could only stare helplessly at him, but she was aware of the whispered speculation from the other journalists.

'Eden Lawrence—she wrote for one of the big nationals, didn't she? She was caught up in some military coup in Africa a couple of years ago.'

'Yeah, but didn't she have an affair with Santini…?'

She really needed to get out of here, Eden thought desperately, and then suddenly two security guards materialised on either side of her and she faced the utter humiliation of being escorted from the conference hall under the brooding gaze of the one man she had hoped to avoid at all costs.

'Come this way.'

It was a demand rather than a request, and it was easier to go gracefully than cause a scene. What on earth had induced her to come within a ten-mile radius of Rafael Santini? she thought bleakly as she marched alongside the security guards, her head held high, hiding the fact that inside she felt sick with mortification. She should never have listened to Cliff, never have allowed him to persuade her to attend the Press conference when there was even the slightest risk that she would meet Rafe again.

She couldn't blame Cliff, she admitted painfully. She had been unable to resist the chance to see Rafe again after all these years, but if she had been testing her immunity to him, she'd failed miserably.

Coming here today hadn't been a wise move, she acknowledged as she stepped into the hotel foyer and headed for the door. Immediately, one of the security guards put a hand on her arm and she found herself being guided firmly towards the lift.

'Do you mind?' she demanded icily. 'You've done your job and I'd like to leave now.'

'Excuse?' the guard said with a shrug, although she was damned sure he had understood her. But as she tried to pull free she found that she had been cleverly manoeuvred into the lift. 'Signor Santini will see you in his suite.'

'The heck he will!' The elevator door opened as they arrived at the top floor and the guard who had been holding her arm stood aside to usher her out, but Eden refused to budge and she glared at him belligerently. The security guards were big and, if she was honest, intimidating, but she had had plenty of dealings with henchmen and refused to be cowed. 'You can tell Signor Santini I have no wish to see him.'

'Excuse?' The shrug was almost comical, very Mediterranean, and Eden felt her temper flare.

'Tell Signor Santini…'

'Why don't you tell him yourself?'

Eden hadn't noticed the arrival of the other lift, but suddenly Rafe appeared in the corridor, tall, dark and indecently good-looking. Her heart performed a painful summersault in her chest as she caught sight of him, and some basic instinct for self-preservation saw her scrabble for the button to close the lift door. One handcrafted Italian leather shoe prevented its closure, the smile that split his features so reminding her of a wolf about to devour its prey that she actually backed up against the lift wall.

'Well, well; Eden Lawrence,' he drawled in his strongly accented English. 'The most surprising things crawl out of the woodwork!' he added silkily, and she shivered at the bitter contempt in his voice. An elderly couple was hovering in the corridor behind him and he smiled warmly at them. 'Out you come, Eden, you're holding these nice people up,' he murmured.

He could turn on the charm the way other people could turn on a light switch, Eden thought grimly as she found that she had no choice but to step into the corridor, the guards moving to stand on either side of her.

As soon as Rafe had pressed the button to close the lift doors she rounded on him. 'You can call off your bully-boys. It was bad enough that you had me frogmarched out of the Press conference without them dragging me up here.'

Dark eyes flicked from her to the two guards and he spoke to them in voluble Italian that was too quick for her to pick out more than a couple of words. 'You exaggerate, Eden,' he said when he turned his attention back to her. 'Paolo and Romano assure me that they treated you with the utmost respect.' His tone and the sardonic gleam in his eyes told her it was a respect he believed to be undeserved and she flushed as he opened the door to his suite. He stood aside to usher her inside but Eden stood firm and lifted her chin, her indignation palpable.

'I won't come in; I'm not stopping.'

Rafe's black brows lifted quizzically. 'Yet you came to the hotel especially to see me?'

No change in his supreme self-confidence, Eden thought darkly, although, to be fair, why should there be? Women had thrown themselves at him for as long as he could remember, but she was determined not to make the same mistake twice. 'As arrogant as ever, Rafe,' she remarked coolly, 'but I'm afraid the only reason I came was that Cliff Harley asked me to attend the Press conference and write an article for my old paper.'

'I see,' Rafe murmured dulcetly, and Eden hoped that he didn't. He had always possessed an uncanny knack of being able to read her mind, but she had been younger then and not as skilled at hiding her emotions. 'Now that you're here, at least allow me to offer you a drink. You look,' he paused, his brows raised in sardonic amusement, 'hot, and you seem to have spilt something down your trousers.'

Instantly, Eden felt as though she was burning up. She knew her cheeks must be flaming, and a glance at her cream linen trousers revealed a dark stain that ran halfway down her thigh. 'It's coffee,' she muttered, 'courtesy of the idiot I was sitting next to. If it hadn't been for him pouring boiling liquid into my lap, you would never have known I was in the conference hall.'

'I knew you were there,' Rafe told her shortly as he indicated that she should take a seat on one of the plush leather sofas. 'What would you like—wine, juice, tea?' he added, obviously remembering her fondness for a cup of tea.

'Orange juice will be fine,' Eden replied hastily. Hot tea would take too long to drink when she was desperate to escape, and she certainly couldn't handle Rafe and alcohol— she needed to keep a clear head. 'What do you mean, you knew I was there? How could you possibly have known?'

'I felt your presence,' Rafe answered simply. 'If you hadn't drawn attention to yourself I would have scoured the room until I found you.'

A heavy silence filled the room and Eden stared at the carpet, studying the intricate gold and beige pattern with apparent fascination while she fought to control the frantic thud of her heart. He was so gorgeous and she had been starved of him for so long. Her eyes kept straying to him, tracing the outline of his strong jaw and the hard planes of his face, hovering for an infinitesimal second on the sensual curve of his mouth.

'You should check that the coffee didn't burn your leg,' he told her as he handed her a glass of blessedly cold juice. 'There's a spare robe in the bathroom. You can wear it while I have your trousers laundered.'

'No, it's fine, thanks.' Eden spluttered on her drink at the mere thought of sitting here with Rafe for however long it would take to have her trousers cleaned.

'But if you don't act quickly, your trousers may be ruined.'

'So I'll buy another pair. Leave it, Rafe,' she ordered when he opened his mouth to argue. 'We haven't met for almost four years, and I've no intention of taking my clothes off in the first five minutes.'

'How long do you need—ten minutes, fifteen? I remember a time when you were only too willing to strip off,' he added unforgivably, ignoring her gasp of outrage as he leaned back on the sofa opposite her, his arms outstretched along the back, one ankle hooked over the other thigh in a position of indolent ease.

Photographs did not do him justice, nor did her memories

of him, and the image she had kept locked in her subconscious for the last four years faded to a shadow before his forceful presence. Nothing had prepared her for his raw, provocative sex appeal, a magnetism that reached across the space between them and trapped her in his spell. His mocking taunts instantly catapulted her back in time, so that she glared at him, pushing away the memories.

'That was a long time ago when I was young and naive, although you dispensed with my innocence pretty quickly, didn't you, Rafe?' One look from those smouldering dark eyes and she'd fallen like a skittle, she remembered despairingly. 'I didn't stand a chance against the great Rafael Santini, did I?' she said bitterly, remembering her humiliating eagerness to fall into his arms and bed.

'You were an avid pupil,' Rafe replied coolly, 'so good that you decided to turn your attentions to my brother.' The barely leashed savagery in his voice shook her. The poison was still there, festering, and she felt a sudden stinging sensation behind her eyelids at the unfairness of his accusation.

'That's a lie…'

'I saw you with my own eyes.' Eyes that were now burning like hot coals as he jumped to his feet and glared at her. 'You and Gianni in each other's arms. Are you telling me that what I saw by the pool was an *illusion*?'

Once she had been afraid of his hot temper. Not that she feared he would be violent, never that, but he possessed a cruel tongue and his angry words had flayed her alive.

'I'm not telling you anything,' she replied calmly, refusing to be cowed. 'Why should I waste my breath? You wouldn't listen to me four years ago and I don't suppose you're any more reasonable now.' Four years ago she had been so unsure of herself, so in awe of him, but not anymore. In the space of five minutes he'd tried her, acted as judge and jury and condemned her and she was damned if she would let him see that she was still serving a life sentence.

'*Reasonable!* I caught you half naked in my brother's arms—did you really expect me to be reasonable?' His fury was blistering and directed solely at her, black eyes flashing fire, and Eden felt her own temper flare. She didn't want to be drawn into a slanging match and certainly didn't want to open up old wounds that were still raw even after all this time.

After piercing her with another furious glare, Rafe paced the room, raking his hand through his thick black hair that had the tendency to curl at the nape despite the fact that he kept it cropped uncompromisingly short. She had loved his hair, loved running her fingers through it, holding his head and drawing his mouth down to hers. The memory was so stark it hurt and she bit back a gasp as she tore her eyes from his broad shoulders. She didn't want to remember anything and for the sake of her self-preservation, she needed to get out of his room.

'It was a long time ago,' she murmured, deliberately lowering her voice in an effort to prevent one of Rafe's typical Latin outbursts. 'Time has moved on and so have I.' Not that it felt like it, she thought dismally. Right now she felt as young and immature as she had done when she had met him for the first time five years ago. That first meeting had also taken place in a hotel, but then, far from wanting to avoid him, she had actually shinned up a drainpipe and had clambered through the window of his suite to land in an ungainly heap at his feet.

Despite everything she felt her lips twitch at the memory and Rafe threw her a questioning look.

'Something amuses you?' he queried in his heavily accented English, and Eden swallowed and felt goose-pimples prickle her skin. If anything, his voice was sexier than she remembered, rich and sensuous, licking over her like molten chocolate.

'I was just remembering the first time we met,' she explained huskily. 'Your room was on the second floor and I climbed up to it by hanging on to a drainpipe and some rather unsafe ivy.'

'It was the third floor,' Rafe replied with a slight shudder, 'and I have never forgotten the mental image I had of you lying smashed and broken on the gravel below, had you fallen.'

Eden blinked back the tears that were still threatening to embarrass her. He didn't have to sound as if he had cared, dammit, when she had irrefutable proof that he had never had any feelings for her other than desire. 'I can't imagine what you thought of me,' she muttered, shaking her head as memories crowded back. She had fallen in through the window and been helped to her feet by Rafael Santini, Formula 1 World Champion and the man she had been so eager to meet, but one look into his dark, flashing eyes had rendered her speechless and she had stared up at him, unable to disguise her admiration for his stunning good looks.

He had been twenty-eight and at the peak of physical fitness, which had no doubt helped him win the champion-ship for the third successive year. That, and a competitive spirit that bordered on obsessive, his ruthless determination to win awarding him a hero status that others could only aspire to. His life away from the racetrack was as legendary as his driving skill and hardly a week went by without him featuring in a newspaper or glossy magazine, his love life exposed in minute detail. He had been successful, sophisticated and drop-dead gorgeous and she hadn't stood a chance against his sexy Italian charm.

'I thought you were beautiful.' The softness of Rafe's voice brought her head up and she stared at him, her pulse racing so that she felt breathless and annoyingly disconcerted. 'You were different from any other woman I had met,' he continued, ignoring the expression on her face that told him she was aware of just how different she'd been compared to his usual diet of glamour models, who were an intrinsic part of the Formula 1 scene. 'You were very sweet, very shy and yet utterly determined. You risked your life to climb up to my room, only to inform me that you were not a fan and had only wanted to meet me because of your brother.'

Eden hid her embarrassment with a smile that tilted her wide mouth at the corners, and Rafe's eyes narrowed as he remembered the touch of that mouth beneath his, the taste of her. 'Simon was a devoted fan,' she agreed, 'and I'd promised him I would try and get your autograph, even if I couldn't persuade you to come to the open day of the spinal-injury unit.' Even then, security surrounding the heir to the Santini millions had been tight and the receptionist at the front desk had coldly informed Eden that Signor Santini would see no one, certainly not a junior reporter from the local paper. But the receptionist had been unaware that beneath Eden's meek exterior lurked a will of iron.

'But you did persuade me,' Rafe pointed out and she nodded, recalling her stunned surprise and Simon's excitement when the world's most revered sporting hero had turned up at the open day. It hadn't been a fleeting visit either, Eden remembered. Rafe had stayed all afternoon and spent hours chatting to the children and teenagers who shared a common bond of being confined to a wheelchair. Simon had spoken about Rafe's visit for weeks after and lined his bedroom walls with yet more posters of his hero, pictures that Eden had found herself staring at whenever she had the opportunity.

At sixteen Simon had spent half his life as a paraplegic after he had fallen out of a tree and broken his spine. He might not have been able to walk but he had made up for that by talking, laughing and bringing such joy to everyone he met that Eden's eyes burned at the memory.

'Does Simon still attend the centre?' Rafe asked. 'I gave a donation but I didn't see him at Greenacres.'

'No.' Eden swallowed hard. 'Simon died of heart failure a few months after we…after I…'

'After you cheated on me with my own brother,' Rafe finished bluntly, and the bitterness in his voice shook her. 'It must have been devastating for all of you, particularly your mother; I remember how devoted she was to him.'

Eden nodded. 'Losing Simon was one of the reasons Dad took up the post of pastor at the missionary church in Africa. He thought that going somewhere where he and my mother were so needed would help her come to terms with Simon's death.' She stared at her lap, fighting the rush of tears, and when she looked up she discovered that Rafe was watching her, a curious expression on his face.

'I know how hard it is,' he offered quietly. 'I too have lost a brother.'

Remorse instantly flooded through her at her insensitivity. 'I was so sorry to hear about Gianni. The accident…it was terrible; I felt so bad for both of you.'

'So bad that you didn't even bother to call,' Rafe taunted, and this time there was no mistaking the anger that darkened his eyes to the colour of jet. '*Madre de Dio*, Eden! You had been close to him, yet you couldn't even be bothered to send a card.'

'That's not fair,' Eden whispered. 'I came to the hospital. I flew to Italy as soon as I heard the news about Gianni's crash.'

The hard stare Rafe gave her spoke plainly of his disbelief. 'You're lying. It was in all the papers that Gianni's injuries were so severe that he would never walk again. You of all people must have realised the hell he was in, especially after you'd lived through it with your own brother. You just didn't want to get involved once you'd heard that Gianni had been left paralysed.' The contempt was back, his black eyes cold and hard as he stared at her, and Eden felt sick at the injustice of his accusation.

'I came to the hospital,' she insisted forcibly, leaning forwards in her desperation to have him believe her. 'I met your father and he said…' She broke off, recalling the unpleasant meeting with Fabrizzio Santini, in which he had made his opinion of her as clear as the fact that she was an unwelcome visitor. 'It doesn't matter what he said,' she muttered, 'it's enough to say he persuaded me that my presence at the hospital wouldn't be welcomed by Gianni and especially not by you.'

'My father made no mention of a visit,' Rafe snapped furiously, his tone so disbelieving that she gave up.

'I don't know why Fabrizzio didn't mention my visit, although I imagine he had his own reasons for not doing so.'

'Meaning what?' Rafe growled.

'Meaning that I'm not a liar! I did go to the hospital. I hoped to see you as well as Gianni. I thought you might need someone to talk to,' she added thickly, remembering the fevered media accusations that Rafe had caused the accident that had left his brother paralysed.

'Did you really think I would talk to you after everything that had happened?' Rafe bit out, his face a taut mask, his olive skin stretched over prominent cheekbones. '*Dio!* Apart from anything else, you're a journalist!' From his tone of voice she might as well have been a mass murderer, but the media had snatched on the rumour that he had caused his brother's accident and had written such scurrilous lies about him that she supposed he had good reason to loathe all members of the Press.

'I went to Italy as a friend, not in my professional capacity,' Eden replied steadily, ignoring the pain around her heart. 'But obviously I was mistaken and you didn't need me at all.'

Silence fell, a silence that thrummed with tension, and Eden set down her glass. It was time to leave. She stood and picked up her handbag, her body stiffening as a door at the far end of the room opened and a woman strolled into the lounge.

'Rafe, darling, I thought I heard you. Are you going to be much longer? I've been waiting for you all morning.'

The pout was pure drama, but the woman was stunning,

Eden acknowledged bleakly, and then derided herself for caring. Rafe had always had his pick of the world's most beautiful girls and he picked with a regularity that reinforced his reputation as a stud. Through the doorway she could see an enormous unmade bed, the tangled sheets and the opened champagne bottle standing in the ice bucket indubitable proof that Rafe still didn't need much sleep.

Memories she believed she had ruthlessly erased forced their way into her mind, memories of another time, of endless hotels where she would spend the days sitting around the pool vainly trying to evoke interest in yet another paperback while she waited for Rafe. The nights had been a different matter, Rafe was a skilled and energetic lover and when she had been in his arms, lost in the exquisite pleasure he wrung from her body, she had almost convinced herself that the lonely days and her loss of self-respect were worthwhile.

'Rafe!' The woman's voice had an edge of petulance, her accent unmistakably Scandinavian, and Rafe threw her an impatient glare.

'I'm busy, Misa; leave us, please.'

With a toss of ash-blonde hair, the woman flounced into the bedroom, slamming the door behind her to emphasise her displeasure.

'Don't ask her to go on my account,' Eden murmured coolly. 'I have another appointment. I take it she's your latest Press officer,' she couldn't resist adding, recalling the job description Rafe had once used as a lure for her to join the Santini team. The glorified title had been nothing more than a smokescreen for her real position as his mistress, and evidently nothing had changed.

Briskly, she walked towards the door but as she reached for the handle she found that Rafe had beaten her to it and the brief contact with his hand sent a jolt of electricity through her so that she instantly dropped her arm.

'Have lunch with me?' The invitation seemed to have been dragged from his soul, his expression thunderous, and she wondered why he had asked when they patently had nothing to say to one another. This close, she was aware of the subtle musk of his aftershave. Heat emanated from his body and curled around her, stirring her senses, and her heart thudded painfully in her chest, so loud she was sure he could hear it. His gaze was focused on her mouth, his eyes hooded so that she couldn't read his expression, but she knew with sudden, blinding realisation that he wanted to kiss her.

Her tongue darted out to moisten her suddenly dry lips, and the unconscious gesture caused him to tense, the silence between them thrumming with electricity. For one dizzy, terrifying moment she imagined the feel of his mouth on hers, the shattering force of his kiss, but for the sake of her own self-respect she couldn't go there again and she tore her eyes from his face.

'No, thanks; I told you I have another appointment.'

'Cancel it.' His arrogant assumption that she would do so made her hackles rise and she gave him a scathing look.

'I don't do threesomes,' she snapped, with a pointed glance at the bedroom door. 'Anyways, it's not an appointment exactly—I'm meeting a friend for lunch.'

Rafe's eyebrows rose quizzically. 'Who is he?' he demanded arrogantly, and Eden glared at him.

'I don't know why you assume it has to be a man, but his

name's Neville Monkton, he owns an estate-agency business in Wellworth.'

'Not to mention an enormous pile called Monkton Hall,' Rafe drawled.

'How on earth do you know that?'

'I know a lot of things,' he told her coolly. 'Is that the reason for your interest, Eden—you fancy becoming lady of the manor?' He paused for a heartbeat before murmuring, 'Does he have a brother?'

'I don't know,' she blinked at him dazedly. 'Why?'

His smile chilled her soul and she shivered at the savage bitterness in his eyes. 'I think I should warn him that you like to keep things in the family,' he murmured silkily, and her fury exploded, her hand lifting, but he caught it before it made contact with his cheek. 'You seem to have developed a temper, *cara*, but then you were never the sweet-natured innocent you had me believe, were you?'

'I was a gullible fool, especially where you were concerned, Rafe. I trusted you but you had your own agenda, didn't you? It was in your interests to believe I was involved with Gianni—that's why you refused to listen to me.' She took a shaky breath and opened the door. 'I was young and painfully naive and you walked all over me, but you won't do so again. I've grown up, Rafe, I've seen you for what you really are, and quite frankly, I'm not impressed!'

CHAPTER TWO

RAFE scoured the ballroom, his smile towards the numerous people who sought to catch his attention barely concealing his impatience. Eden hadn't arrived. Maybe she wasn't coming to the after-race party, although his personal assistant had issued an open invitation to everyone at the local Press office. Maybe she deemed an event to celebrate his win at the British Grand Prix beneath her, he thought darkly as he remembered the cool indifference in her voice when she informed him that she found him to be frankly unimpressive!

Never in his life had he felt so insulted. He was no angel—*Dio*, he was the first to admit that—but he was five times Formula 1 World Champion, he spent his life thrilling packed crowds as he hurtled around a circuit. Yet Eden Lawrence was not impressed. She hadn't been referring to his driving skill. In his heart he knew that, but the fact that she was unimpressed by the man, the real Rafael Santini, sat uncomfortably on his shoulders because she knew him better than most.

He didn't know what he had expected her reaction at seeing him again to be, but a healthy dose of gratitude that he was prepared to overlook the past and speak to her wouldn't have come amiss. The trouble was, he hadn't been able to dismiss the past as easily as he'd thought. Her appearance at the Press conference had startled him. Even though he knew she was back in Wellworth working as a journalist on the local paper he hadn't really expected to see her at the hotel and he'd been unprepared, thrown off balance at the sight of her after all this time. He'd forgotten just how beautiful she was, or maybe not forgotten, just tried to bury the memory of her creamy, satin skin, eyes the colour of the sky on a summer's day and that wide, full mouth. Even now he could feel the softness of her lips beneath his, he could taste her, but every time he closed his eyes he could see her kissing Gianni.

'Rafe, do we have to stand here all night?' Misa pouted prettily and glanced at him appealingly from beneath her lashes in a coquettish gesture that left him cold. After three months their relationship had run its course; all that loomed ahead were the tears and tantrums when he ended it, with the gift of a suitable trinket as recompense, he concluded cynically.

'I'm quite happy standing here,' he replied coolly, his gaze skirting to the ballroom entrance once more, 'but obviously you're free to go where you please.'

'I don't know why you decided to hold the party in this dump anyways,' Misa muttered sulkily. 'Where is Wellworth anyways? It doesn't even have any decent shops.'

Aware that she did not have Rafe's attention, she clung to him and threw back her hair so that her breasts almost escaped the tiny scrap of material that masqueraded as a dress, but to no avail. Rafe's gaze was focused on the woman who had just entered the ballroom.

In contrast to Misa's over-exposed charms, Eden looked as chaste as a nun in a simple navy-blue sheath that skimmed her breasts and hips. The long skirt had a discreet split that revealed one slender leg and when she turned Rafe saw that, although the bodice was high-necked at the front, the back was cut away, leaving an expanse of tantalising, silky skin.

Elegant, sophisticated—Eden had grown up, he conceded, and felt a tug of primitive longing in his gut, so intense it was a physical ache. The most responsive, *generous* lover he had ever known, she wore her sensuality like a cloak, and his feet moved of their own accord towards her, pausing when he noticed that idiot estate agent, Neville Monkton, had beaten him to it. Abruptly he swung away and headed for the group of promotional models who worked for the various sponsors. They at least found him impressive and no way did he want Eden to think he had been waiting for her. If and when he decided to resume their relationship, it would be on his terms, he would be in control, and it was time his rampaging hormones understood that fact.

'Eden, great to see you; you look stunning.'

'Thank you.' Eden smiled as Neville Monkton strolled across the ballroom to greet her. The obvious admiration in his eyes boosted her confidence, which was decidedly shaky. She hadn't wanted to come to the after-race party. She remembered them too well from the year she'd spent with Rafe—but Cliff had pleaded and she hadn't had the heart to refuse him.

'I can't go, not with Jenny about to go into labour any minute,' he'd said. 'A few details about the aftermath of the Grand Prix will round off your article nicely, especially if you can grab an interview with Santini.'

'I can't promise anything,' Eden had muttered, recalling the interview she had already had with Rafael Santini, which was definitely not for public consumption.

The party was exactly as she had expected, the ballroom packed with nubile blondes who made her feel distinctly overdressed. She couldn't see Rafe and had no intention of looking for him; she was through with acting like a lovesick puppy and she smiled warmly at Nev.

'If I'd known you were coming, I'd have offered you a lift,' he said as he led her over to the bar.

'It was a last-minute decision. Jenny was having twinges and Cliff didn't want to leave her. But I didn't drive, I came by taxi.'

'Sensible if you want to have a drink,' Nev agreed, 'but I did bring the car tonight, so I'll give you a lift home.'

Nev was nice, Eden decided as she took a sip of deliciously cold Chardonnay. He was affable and uncomplicated, two of the characteristics she would look for in a man if she ever considered a serious relationship again. She was done with volatile, passionate, sexy Italians. She didn't want a man who would take her to the edge of ecstasy—the inevitable fall was too painful and it had taken her four years to recover.

'It's quite a do,' Nev commented as he eyed the magnificent buffet set out at the far end of the room, 'but I guess Santini can afford it; he must be loaded. Didn't you know him at one time?' he asked curiously and Eden shrugged noncommittally.

'Briefly, a few years ago.'

'What about the brother, Gianni? The news of his death was pretty tragic. They said he couldn't come to terms with being left unable to walk after his accident, and took his own life. Rafe must be gutted, especially as it was rumoured that he caused the accident.'

The fine hairs on the back of her neck prickled and Eden knew with absolute certainty that Rafe was close—she could feel him with every fibre of her body—and for a second she closed her eyes in despair. She didn't want to feel like this, it had taken her a long time to get over him and she wouldn't let one meeting ruin all that hard work.

'I wouldn't believe everything you read in the gutter Press,' she told Nev coolly. 'Rafe wasn't responsible for Gianni's crash; that fact was proved irrefutably.'

'There was an intense rivalry between them though, wasn't there?' Nev pressed. 'I understood they weren't on speaking terms at the time of the accident.'

'They were friends as well as brothers,' Eden said shortly. 'That's all I know.' It was not for her to reveal that alongside the competitive rivalry between the Santini brothers had existed a deep, enduring love that had seen Rafe believe Gianni over her. It was in the past, she reminded herself, fighting the memory of Rafe's furious face and his scathing denouncement of her as a cheap whore who had played him and his brother for fools. She had barely tried to defend herself, too shocked by Gianni's lies to even think straight, and afterwards, on the flight back from Italy, she'd concluded that Rafe had his own reasons for wanting to believe the worst of her. He'd been looking for an excuse to get rid of her.

'Do you fancy something to eat?' Nev asked as he steered her towards the buffet, but one glance at the mountain of food made Eden's stomach churn.

'You go ahead,' she murmured, 'it's too hot in here for me, I'm going out on the terrace for a while.' She swung round and her heart missed a beat as her eyes were drawn to the group standing a little ways off, with Rafe at its epicentre. He was taller than any man in the room but it wasn't just his height and the breadth of his shoulders that drew attention, it was his air of authority, his power and magnificent arrogance. He was the world's number one and it wasn't just his skill on the racetrack that elevated him to hero status. He possessed a charisma that drew people to him, men and women alike, although inevitably it was women who surrounded him now, the usual array of groupies who were fawning over him while he took their attention as his God-given right. He glanced over at that moment, and she flushed at the sardonic amusement in his eyes that told her he was aware of her scrutiny. She swallowed and hastily dropped her gaze as he dipped his head in a silent, mocking greeting, and, dragging her eyes from him, she headed for the door to the terrace.

The night air was cool on Eden's skin, the mingled scent of honeysuckle and roses soothing her until a familiar voice shattered her peace.

'All alone, Eden? Where's your faithful lapdog?'

No man had the right to look so decadently sexy, she thought bleakly as she sought to control her racing pulse. His black silk shirt emphasised the width of his shoulders, the top couple of buttons left unfastened to reveal the gold chain around his neck. He looked every inch the stud he was reputed to be, she decided with a grimace that she convinced herself was of distaste, not jealousy of all the women who had shared his bed. Wealth and magnetic sex appeal combined with stunning looks; Rafe had it all and she very much doubted that he had spent the last four years celibate. He'd been her first and only lover, but to him she had been just another notch on the bedpost. Why, then, did her subconscious cling to the belief that she was his woman, and why did her body instantly react to his presence as if she had been waiting and longing for him all this time?

'If you're referring to Nev, he's inside and he's hardly my lapdog. I don't even know him that well. He's a friend, that's all.'

'Not to mention the owner of Monkton Hall,' Rafe murmured silkily. 'Are you sure you're not aiming to become the lady of the manor, Eden?'

'You've already made that insulting suggestion, but to be honest I really don't see that it has anything to do with you,' Eden snapped, taking a step backwards when she realised how close Rafe was standing. For such a big man he moved with the stealth of a big cat, silent, menacing, waiting to pounce. Looking at him was a mistake, she realised as her breath snagged in her throat. If anything it was even worse than this morning, this awareness of him, this recognition of her soul mate. He was not her soul mate, her mind screamed. One-time bed mate, that was all he had ever been, but out here on the shadowed terrace the moonlight seemed to be mirrored in his eyes, calling her, drawing her back to him.

'So tell me, *cara*,' Rafe murmured, his deliciously husky accent shivering across her skin, 'if you're not back in Wellworth to snag a rich husband, what are you doing? You gained a reputation as a respected journalist with your work in Africa; why settle for a job with the local rag?'

'I need a break,' Eden admitted quietly, her eyes shadowed. 'The last three years have been…hard.' Culminating in the land-mine explosion that had nearly blown away her left leg, although she refused to reveal that snippet of information to Rafe. After he had ended their relationship so savagely she had returned to England, determined to bury herself in her career, and had been lucky enough to find a job as a reporter with a national paper. She'd been young, free and single and life in London should have been fun, but she had missed Rafe with a clawing desperation that seemed to get worse with every passing day, and the regular features about his love life in the tabloids hadn't helped. The trip to Africa to visit her parents had seemed a good way of exorcising him from her mind; she hadn't known that it would change her life.

The poverty she had witnessed had been appalling, even before the military coup that had plunged the area into a violent battleground, and there certainly hadn't been time to think of anything other than basic survival. Afterwards, when some semblance of peace returned, she had stayed on, so moved by the plight of the gentle people she had met that she had been desperate to help them rebuild their shattered lives. Even now, thinking about them hurt, and the realisation that Rafe believed her to be some sort of gold-digger hurt more.

She took a step back, distancing herself from him mentally as well as physically, and Rafe cursed silently, frantically trying to control the violent emotions that surged through him. 'I read your newspaper reports and saw the documentary you made,' he said huskily as he recalled his feeling of helplessness and his fear for her safety. 'How could you have put yourself in such danger that your life was at risk on a daily basis?' His voice was harsh, rasping over her skin, and she could feel the tension in him, could see it in his eyes, which had darkened with an anger that seemed to be directed at himself. 'If you had been with me I would not have allowed you to go.'

Eden gave a brittle laugh. 'You were the one to end our relationship, Rafe.'

'With good reason, namely that you were screwing my brother!' His temper was at simmering point again; she could see it in the rigid line of his jaw, his eyes burning like hot coals in his hard-boned face. 'I couldn't believe it when a year later I saw the news reports you managed to smuggle out of West Africa. What were you trying to do, atone for your sins? A two-timing harlot transformed into Mother Teresa!'

'You bastard.' Eden swung away from him, blinded by sudden tears that she was determined would not fall. She'd cried a river over Rafe Santini but she was over him; he couldn't hurt her again.

Rafe forced himself to uncurl his clenched fists and laid his hands flat on the low wall that ran the length of the terrace, resisting the urge to shake her. Like thousands of others, he had read the reports that had filtered out of the African state, detailing the violent clashes between opposing groups. He had been horrified by the stories of barbarism inflicted on the local tribespeople caught in the midst of the conflict, but more shocking to him had been the realisation that it was Eden who had been trapped in the area, who had actually been taken hostage at one point and who'd risked her life to smuggle out her reports that alerted the outside world to the crisis. His first instinct had been to save her but he didn't have the right to interfere in her life. He'd ended all involvement with her when he'd bundled her on the first flight back to England after finding her in Gianni's arms, and he'd cursed himself for his weakness as he scanned the television channels in the hope of seeing her face.

Eden spun round to face him and his heart clenched at the over-brightness of her eyes. Beneath that air of sophistication lurked the vulnerability he remembered so well and he fought the urge to pull her into his arms and hold her close.

'I don't have to stay here and listen to your insults. You never would listen, would you, Rafe? You were always so damn sure you were right. But I no longer care what you think; I've nothing to be ashamed of. I know the truth and so did Gianni.' She waited for his anger to break over her, for the caustic words that in the past had tripped so easily from his tongue. His silence shocked her and the shadows in his eyes caused a tug of compassion in her chest. Rafe was hurting. He had loved his brother, and the tragic circumstances of his death must still be an agonising memory.

'What if I was to listen now?' he asked huskily, and for a second her heart stopped beating. 'It's too late to talk to Gianni, but you…'

'You're too late for me, too,' Eden replied, hardening her heart against him although she was breaking up inside. 'Four years too late. So if you've been attacked by a belated sense of guilt you'll just have to suffer, and I hope you do.' As she had, but no more—if Rafe had expected to find the pathetic pushover she had once been, he was in for a shock. It had taken a long time to win back her self-respect and she wasn't about to lose it, however much her heart ached for him.

He tensed, his body so still that he looked as if he had been carved from stone, his eyes hooded and unfathomable, but then suddenly he relaxed and shrugged as if he couldn't give a damn, which most probably he didn't, she conceded bleakly.

'The little kitten has developed into a she-cat—with claws,' he murmured, and she caught the note of amusement in his voice. 'I don't remember you being so argumentative, *cara*.'

'And didn't you take advantage of my insecurity?' she flung at him bitterly. 'You knew I was in awe of you. I couldn't believe that the great Rafael Santini wanted to be with *me*, a dull little innocent from a sleepy English village. You must have loved the fact that I was desperate to keep you happy.'

'I loved the fact that you were desperate for me,' he mocked, and she flinched as he trailed a finger lightly over her cheekbone, down her neck to rest against the pulse that jerked frenetically at the base of her throat. He was so beautiful. She had forgotten the sheer impact of his height and the width of his shoulders, but time had done nothing to erase the memory of that sensual mouth on hers and she shivered, her senses on fire as she caught the exotic scent of his cologne. Frantically, she pulled herself free of his hold.

'So the sex was good. You certainly deserved your reputation as a stud, Rafe, but our relationship was based on nothing more than that.'

His eyes narrowed, glinting dangerously as he drawled, 'Don't knock it, *cara*. Maybe we should give it another go?'

He couldn't be serious, *could he*? The worst of it was she

was tempted; even after all he'd put her through. She must need her head tested, she acknowledged as she sought to put some space between them before she did something utterly stupid like throw herself into his arms. 'Never in this lifetime,' she snapped, and he gave a lazy smile.

It would be satisfying to make her eat her words, to close the gap between them, tilt her chin and plunder the tremulous softness of her mouth. Her resistance would be minimal, he knew it as well as she, but it was the faint edge of desperation in her eyes that had him fight the urge to show her that in some things at least, nothing had changed. The sexual chemistry that existed between them was as fierce as ever.

He missed her, he acknowledged grimly. Despite coming close to hating her, to telling himself that she was a lying, cheating bitch, he still woke every morning in the hour before dawn and reached for her, and the realisation that she was no longer there never failed to hurt.

'Out of interest,' she queried as she paused in the doorway leading to the ballroom, 'what are you doing in Wellworth? The Bembridge is an excellent hotel but there are others as good and a lot closer to Silverstone.'

'You don't think it possible that I came to find you?' he murmured lightly and she gave a harsh laugh.

'Unlikely; according to the last time we met, I'm a two-timing whore. Why on earth would you come looking for me?'

'Maybe I missed you, *cara mia*,' he suggested softly and she steeled herself against the insidious warmth his words evoked.

'It's more likely that you've run out of women to sleep

with, but whatever your reasons, Rafe, I'm not interested. No doubt you'll be leaving Wellworth tomorrow and for all I care you can go to hell. It's where I've been for the last four years.'

Neville Monkton glanced up as she rejoined him in the ballroom, frowning as he noted her white face.

'Are you OK, Eden? I was just about to send out a search party.'

'Sorry…I've got a thumping headache; I think I'll call a cab.'

'Don't be silly; I'll run you home. I'm ready to leave anyways.'

'It's been a good day,' he told her cheerfully as he steered down the narrow lane to her parents' cottage. 'You know the Dower House, at the far end of the village? A couple of property developers bought it a year ago and have completely renovated it. It's been on my letting books for the last two months and I heard today that I've found a tenant.'

Eden smiled faintly and tried to sound interested although her headache was now a throbbing reality. 'Who's renting it—a family? It's certainly big enough.'

Nev shook his head. 'A business consortium have taken it; they'll probably use it as a base for visiting executives, but, to be honest, for the rent they've agreed to, I don't care if they move a circus in. How did the interview with Rafe Santini go?' he asked as he pulled up in front of the cottage. 'You were outside on the terrace with him for a long time; did you get what you wanted?

'I didn't learn anything new,' Eden replied quietly as she climbed out of the car. She wasn't going to reveal to Nev the one vital fact she'd learned tonight. She was still reeling from the shock of discovering that her much-vaulted belief that she was over Rafe was not as assured as she'd hoped. Seeing him again had been devastating; he'd trampled down her carefully erected barricades with frustrating ease and she was going to have her work cut out reassembling them.

CHAPTER THREE

EDEN watched the removal van disappear from sight before she wandered back into the empty cottage. The past couple of days had been spent in a haze of frantic activity as she organised the packing of her parents' furniture and belongings, but now everything was stowed safely on the lorry that was heading for Scotland.

All that remained was for her to pack her own few possessions before she moved into the flat Nev had found for her to rent. While her parents had been house-hunting in Edinburgh, having decided to move nearer to her elderly grandmother, Eden had overseen the sale of their cottage. The new owner's request to take possession at the beginning of July had been a shock, and meant she only had a few days to organise her own move.

The flat was on a new housing estate on the outskirts of the village. It wasn't her first choice, but property in the pretty Oxfordshire village was expensive to rent and taking on a mortgage on her current salary was out of the question. Her only other choice was to relocate to London and look for a better-paid job with one of the national papers. Her reputation as a dedicated and fearless journalist would stand her in good stead, but the three years she'd spent in Africa had left her emotionally and physically drained.

She loved Wellworth. It had been her home for most of her life and she had happy memories of growing up in the vicarage, an idyllic, if rather sheltered childhood that had left her ill-prepared for the world outside—unprepared for Rafe Santini, that was for sure, she brooded as she made a cup of tea. He'd swept into her life like a whirlwind and she had been utterly overwhelmed by his charm. He was different from any other man she had met, although admittedly there hadn't been many, just a couple of fledgling romances while she was at university.

Rafe had surprised and delighted her when he had arrived at the open day of the spinal-injury unit her brother, Simon, attended, and she'd suffered a serious dose of hero worship, but never in her wildest dreams had she expected him to turn up at the vicarage to ask her out to dinner.

Angrily, she searched through the packing boxes for the teapot as memories plagued her. Perhaps it would be a good idea to move away from Wellworth. A fresh start in London, where there were no reminders of Rafe, might be just what she needed. What she didn't need was the vivid mental image of the first time he had made love to her, his gentle sensitivity when he had discovered she was a virgin and his rather endearing smug satisfaction when he told her she was his woman and his alone.

God damn it! Why couldn't he stay in the past instead of haunting her every waking thought and dominating her dreams? She snatched up her mug of tea and stormed out of the kitchen, only to cannon into something hard and solid and intoxicatingly warm.

'Rafe! What on earth are you doing here? How did you get in?' Acute shock added fuel to her temper and she glared at him furiously. It was bad enough that he was inside her head without finding him a few centimetres in front of her.

'The front door was open. You should be more careful, *cara*; anyone could walk in.'

'Anyone just did, although, to be honest, Jack the Ripper would be preferable. Why are you here, Rafe? I assumed you would be on the other side of the world by now.'

The coldness of her voice warned him that, as far as she was concerned, another planet would be too close, and his lips twitched. There was a new feistiness about her that hadn't been there five years ago. She'd been younger then, he reminded himself, sweet-natured and desperately shy. It had taken every ounce of his patience to persuade her into his bed, but she'd been worth the wait. For a brief moment he closed his eyes and pictured the whiteness of her skin, her firm, full breasts with their pink, acutely sensitive peaks that he loved to suckle. His arousal was instant and embarrassingly hard and he crossed his arms over his chest in the hope of drawing her attention away from his jeans, which were suddenly un-comfortably tight.

'The Canadian Grand Prix isn't for another two weeks,' he informed her. 'I thought I might spend some time in Wellworth.'

'I can't think why—it's hardly Monte Carlo. There's nothing for you to get excited about here.'

'You underestimate yourself, *cara*. I find certain elements in Wellworth highly exciting.'

'Oh, for heaven's sake!' Verbal seduction she could do

without. She couldn't imagine why Rafe was here or what he was up to other than playing a game of cat and mouse, but she refused to award him the satisfaction of knowing that he was getting to her, or that her heart was racing like a steam train. She stomped into the living room, uncaring if he followed or not, and settled on the wide windowsill, which had to suffice as a chair now that all the furniture had gone.

'*Dio!* Have you been burgled?' Rafe's face was a picture as his gaze trawled the empty room and hovered on the torn wallpaper that had been behind the sofa. 'No wonder you're interested in the wealthy squire if you have to live like this.'

'My parents have just sold the cottage and I'm about to move into a flat,' Eden snapped, her patience paper-thin. 'I'm not interested in Nev or anyone else. Have you ever heard the expression "once bitten, twice shy"? Believe me, Rafe, you've put me off relationships for life. I'll never trust another man again.' Or hand over her heart with a naive trust that made her weep just thinking about how gullible she had been.

'Trust!' Rafe threw the word at her, a nerve jumping in his cheek as he sought to control the wave of fury that swept through him. 'You dare speak to me of trust when you shattered mine,' he demanded, his accent suddenly very pronounced. 'You ripped my heart out! I gave you everything including my *trust* and you flung it back in my face.'

Gone was the urbane, charming Rafael Santini he portrayed to the world, in his place a fiery, hot-tempered Italian. He was unlike anyone she had ever met and his volatile outbursts had secretly fascinated her, especially when his anger had so often evaporated as quickly as it came, to be replaced with a passion that shook her with its intensity.

'Tell me, Eden, what would you have thought if you had caught me by the poolside, half naked and in the arms of another woman? Add to that the fact that you were kissing my own brother, a man I trusted beyond any other, and what would your reaction have been in similar circumstances?'

'I would have at least listened,' Eden muttered numbly. She'd never looked at it from his point of view and, if she was honest, the sight of him with another woman would have sent her running, desperately seeking sanctuary to lick her wounded pride. But she had always expected the worst, always assumed that he would one day tire of her ordinariness and replace her. She'd never given him cause to doubt her, with Gianni or anyone else. She'd been too hooked on Rafe, and her wide-eyed adoration was a humiliating memory she preferred to forget.

'I did listen,' Rafe stated forcefully, needing to assure himself of that fact as well as her. In all honesty the sight of her slender bikini-clad body in his brother's arms had made him feel so sick he'd barely heard anything other than the splintering of his heart. 'I listened to your silence while Gianni explained how you had made all the running, until he'd been unable to resist you.'

'And you believed him,' Eden said quietly.

'He was my brother,' Rafe roared, black eyes flashing fire as he paced the empty room that seemed claustrophobically small with him in it. 'Why would he lie?'

'I don't know.' No one would, now; Gianni was dead and had taken his reasons for wrecking her relationship with Rafe with him. She couldn't even blame Gianni entirely. The relationship had already been doomed and Rafe must have been searching for a reason to end it—either that or he really had intended to keep her as his mistress after his marriage to the daughter of an Italian aristocrat.

'It's all immaterial now,' she muttered, wondering how he dared to sound so *hurt* when she had been the one who had been betrayed, who'd had her heart broken into so many pieces that she was still trying to superglue it back together. 'I don't know what you hoped to achieve by coming here.'

Rafe took a deep breath and raked his hand through his hair, aware that the meeting wasn't going as planned. 'I came to offer you my forgiveness,' he informed her with a haughtiness that hid his growing realisation that he was on shaky ground.

He sounded like a statesman making a royal proclamation and, even taking into account his strong accent, there was no disguising the arrogance of his tone. Eden set down the mug of rapidly cooling tea before she spilt it, or threw it at his head. He was waiting, silently watching her with an air of expectancy that made her wonder what she was supposed to do now. Fall at his feet in abject gratitude most likely, she decided and was filled with a cold fury that was murderous in its intensity.

'That's big of you,' she murmured coolly when she trusted herself to speak, 'but actually, no, thanks.'

'What do you mean, no, thanks?' His look of outraged perplexity would have been funny if she hadn't been so close to tears. 'I've realised that what we had together was worth fighting for. I'm prepared to overlook what happened with Gianni and give our relationship another chance.'

'Well, you've realised four years too late!' Her gentle,

pacifist parents had taught her that anger solved nothing and for years, Eden had stifled her emotions. During the year she'd spent as Rafe's mistress she'd been far too in awe of him to ever argue with him, but she was a different person now. The sights she'd witnessed in Africa, the poverty and inhumanity inflicted on its people, had released a great well of anger as she argued their cause. She was no longer afraid to express her emotions and right now Rafe was in her direct line of fire.

'I don't need your forgiveness; I've done nothing wrong, so if you're waiting for some sort of apology you'll be waiting till kingdom come. The only person who needs to apologise is you,' she continued, her eyes blazing as she jumped up and glared at him. 'The only conniving, two-timing cheat around here is you,' she flung at him as she stabbed her finger into his chest. 'So now I'd like you to leave. Go back to Mitzy or Misty or whatever your latest "Press officer's" name is and leave me in peace!'

For a few seconds Rafe appeared completely poleaxed. He'd never heard her raise her voice before, let alone scream at him like a banshee, Eden acknowledged grimly. But then his frown lifted and he actually had the audacity to smile as he murmured, 'I have already ended my affair with Misa. You have no reason to be jealous, *cara.*'

Eden inhaled deeply, her chest heaving, although her voice dripped ice. 'I'm sure your *wife* will be very relieved but I really couldn't care less and I'm certainly not jealous. I'd rather sell my soul to the devil than take another chance on you.'

She had to get away from him before she burst into tears or, even more humiliatingly, flung herself against his chest and begged for the second chance he said he was offering. He stared down at her like an avenging angel, his superbly chiselled features so rigid with tension that he could have been sculpted from marble, and she remembered with stark clarity the feel of that sensual mouth on hers. How could she turn down the chance to experience the exquisite mastery of his possession? He was the love of her life; the bleak emptiness of the last four years were proof of that. But he didn't love her, never had, and she wouldn't sacrifice her self-respect for sex again, however good. She was worth more than that.

'What do you mean, my wife? *Madre de Dio!* I don't have a wife,' Rafe ground out, gripping her arm as she tried to push past him.

'So what happened to Valentina de Domenici, the woman you were intending to marry? I know about her, Rafe. I know that a marriage between the two of you had been arranged by your father years before, and that you were planning to keep me tucked away as your mistress after you'd made Valentina your wife. It was a disgusting plan then and four years on it doesn't look any more inviting.' In her desperation to get away she struggled to pull free of his bruising hold. 'Let go, Rafe; you're hurting me.'

'You know nothing,' Rafe snarled furiously. 'What is this nonsense, Eden—some pathetic attempt to shift the blame? It won't work, *cara. Dio!* I used to watch you flirt with Gianni but I never suspected you would lead him on to such an extent that he could no longer fight his desire for you.'

'Rafe, my arm…' Eden pleaded and he glanced down to where his fingers were biting into her flesh before releasing her with a savage oath in his native tongue.

'I should have listened to my father,' he muttered darkly. 'He warned me about you.'

'I bet he did...he never liked me. He thought I wasn't good enough for you.'

'That's a ridiculous thing to say.' Rafe's gaze skittered away and Eden sighed. Why was she even bothering to fight a battle she knew she would lose? In the year that she had spent with Rafe, Fabrizzio Santini had barely acknowledged her presence, and, as she only ever met him at the racetrack, where nerves were stretched and the tension thrumming, his rudeness towards her went unnoticed, by everyone but her. Later, when she had rushed to the hospital after Gianni's accident, Fabrizzio had bluntly informed her that she would not be welcomed by any of the Santini family. She had been Rafe's whore, he told her, and she had served her purpose; Rafe had moved on.

Suddenly she felt bone weary. Her relationship with Rafe had happened a long time ago and, as Fabrizzio had pointed out, Rafe had moved on, life had moved on and the fact that her heart was trapped in a time warp was no one's fault but her own. 'There's no point in rehashing the past,' she said quietly. 'Let's just accept that it was good while it lasted.'

'So good that you have never been able to forget it.' He was so close that she had to tip her head to look into his eyes and to her shame, his burning gaze caused an answering heat to flood through her veins.

'Your arrogance never fails to take my breath away,' she snapped, mortified that her voice sounded so husky and unsure when she had been determined to be cool and controlled.

'Not arrogance; it's the truth, for both of us. I have never forgotten you, or what we had together.'

She would not be lured by the sweet seduction of his words, Eden assured herself, fighting the quiver of response that ran the length of her spine. 'We had sex,' she stated bluntly, watching as his mouth curved into a knowing smile. 'And in the years that we've been apart I'm damn sure you've had sex with hundreds of other women. Do you think I didn't notice the groupies that used to hang around the track, waiting for you to beckon?'

'None were as good as you,' he assured her, his black eyes gleaming with amusement, and something else. 'And as for taking your breath away…'

She had been focusing so hard on his words that for a few seconds she didn't realise his intentions, and he made good use of the time to pull her into his arms, his mouth coming down on hers with a force that rendered her helpless. It was no gentle caress, no subtle persuasion in acknowledgement of the years apart, but a brutal assault on her senses, fierce and hot, demanding a response she was unable to deny.

It was like finding heaven after a very long journey, Eden thought numbly, and she wondered how she had survived this long without him. The stroke of his tongue as he probed between her lips splintered the last vestige of her control and as she opened her mouth she heard him groan with a mixture of triumph and growing hunger. His fingers threaded through her hair, holding her fast, while his other hand roamed the length of her body, down her spine, over her hips and finally up again to the curve of her breast. Eden revelled in his touch and her arms crept up around his neck, but when she felt his fingers slide beneath her T-shirt, she stilled. Patience had never been Rafe's strong point and in the heat of passion he had frequently ignored buttons and fastenings and simply ripped her clothes off. Reality intruded and with it the realisation that she was in Rafe's arms, the one place she had vowed she would never be again.

As if sensing her withdrawal, he lifted his head, his eyes hard and cold, and shame engulfed her as he gripped her wrists and removed her arms from around his neck in a gesture of mocking distaste.

'You always were an easy lay,' he murmured lazily and Eden spun away from him, blinded by tears of rage at her own weakness, her hip bone coming into sharp contact with the windowsill.

'Get out,' she ordered, unable to bring herself to look at him as she ran towards the stairs, 'before I call the police and have you charged with harassment. I don't want or need your forgiveness and, despite your arrogant assumption that you're God's gift to women, I don't want you.'

'Do you want the good news or the bad news?' Nev asked when Eden walked into his estate agency the following morning.

Having spent a sleepless night during which murder and Rafe Santini had featured highly in her thoughts, the last thing she needed was more problems, and she frowned. 'Tell me the worst.'

'The flat on the Cob Tree estate is no longer available to rent.'

'But it was practically agreed,' Eden cried, unable to disguise her panic. 'I've got to be out of the cottage by the weekend.'

'I know,' Nev murmured sympathetically. 'The owners phoned this morning to say they'd received an offer from a buyer that they can't refuse.'

'Oh, God.' Eden rubbed her brow wearily. 'What am I going to do? Cliff said I could move in with him and Jenny if necessary but now the baby has arrived and I don't want to add to their problems.'

'There is one possibility that's cropped up,' Nev told her and she stared at him expectantly.

'You mean a property that I can afford has come onto your books? Is it in Wellworth?'

'Very much so—it's the Dower House, undoubtedly the most attractive property in the village.'

'With a rent to match,' Eden said dismally as hope receded. 'Anyways, I thought you'd already found new tenants.'

'I have, and the business group that has signed the year's lease has asked me to find a housekeeper. I spoke to the chief executive, Hank Molloy,' Nev continued. 'The company he works for is a global organisation and they want the house as a British base for their top executives. Mr Molloy says he's hoping to bring his grandchildren over from Texas at the end of the summer and it'll probably be used at Christmas, but for much of the time the house will be empty. He wants to install a resident housekeeper to keep the place ticking over.'

'But I already have a job on the *Gazette*,' Eden said slowly, 'and I'm a hopeless cook.'

'You wouldn't have to do any cooking, just a bit of laundry, overseeing the cleaning contractors, that sort of thing. It could be the answer to your problems, Eden, not to mention mine. Hank Molloy is an extremely brash American who wants everything done yesterday and when I told him I might have someone suitable in mind he faxed over a contract.'

'So would I be employed by Mr Molloy's company?' Eden queried.

'Yes, but the contract seems fine; the only sticking point I can see is that you'd have to agree to give three months' notice should you want to leave.'

'That's hardly a problem; I'm not going anywhere in a hurry,' Eden murmured drily. 'It sounds too good to be true— I can't help thinking there's a catch.'

'Talk to Mr Molloy yourself,' Nev urged as he punched several digits into his phone and handed it to her. 'Let him reassure you that everything's above board.'

Hank Molloy spoke at the pace of a speeding train but after their conversation Eden felt happier about signing the contract. She felt as though a great weight had been lifted from her shoulders and smiled warmly at Nev. 'You're a star; I don't know how to thank you.'

'For a start you can agree to have dinner with your favourite estate agent,' he teased, and she hesitated for a moment. Nev was a great guy but she wasn't interested and it would be unfair to let him believe they could be anything more than friends. On the other hand it was only dinner, she argued with herself. She'd been so tense since Rafe had turned up to disrupt her emotional stability and she needed something, anything to banish him from her mind.

The Dower House was a listed building that dated back to the eighteenth century. A spacious six-bedroom house set in several acres of Oxfordshire countryside, it had been expertly renovated and refurbished and Eden had fallen in love with it the minute she'd walked through the door. The position of housekeeper was the most incredible piece of luck, she mused as she climbed the central staircase to the pretty guest bedroom she had chosen. She still couldn't help thinking there must be a catch and she wondered when Hank Molloy would visit. She hoped Nev was right and she wouldn't be expected to cook because she was hopeless in the kitchen and could very well find herself out of her new home.

The night was sultry. A thunderstorm had been brewing all day and when she threw open her bedroom window the air was hot and ominously still. The last few days had been tiring, what with packing up her parents' furniture and moving her own possessions into the Dower House, yet she dreaded going to bed. Inactivity gave her time to think and her thoughts turned with relentless inevitability to one man, her fractured dreams haunted by memories of the closeness she and Rafe had once shared. It had been an illusion, she angrily reminded herself. The feeling that he was her other half, the keeper of her soul, had been a figment of her imagination, cruelly shattered the night he'd found her and Gianni by the pool.

Forget him, she told herself. He had doubtless already dismissed her from his mind and was probably on the other side of the world with his Swedish blonde—or her replacement. The emotion in her heart twisted. She reached for the packet of painkillers the hospital had prescribed, her leg was aching— not surprising when it was held together with a series of metal pins. Usually she was able to ignore the dull pain, but tonight she wanted the sanctuary of oblivion and a good night's sleep.

A few hours later she opened her eyes as a brilliant flash lit up the room. The thunder was a low, angry growl that wasn't really loud enough to have woken her and she lay in the darkness, wondering why her skin prickled, her ears straining for the other faint sound she had heard.

An intruder or an overactive imagination? she queried silently, when the definitive thud of the front door closing sounded up the stairs. Sleep was impossible until she'd set her mind to rest but the faint glimmer of light visible from beneath the living-room door caused her heart to pound, and her palms were clammy with sweat as she tiptoed down the stairs. Cursing the fact that she'd left her mobile phone in her bedroom, she acknowledged that her only option was to slip out of the front door and run down the lane to the nearest house for help, but she was in her pyjamas and now it was raining. Suddenly the living-room door swung open and she gasped and grabbed the nearest potential weapon.

'It seems an odd time for flower arranging,' came a familiar husky drawl. 'What on earth are you doing, *cara*?'

'What am *I* doing?' For all of thirty seconds, words failed her as she set the heavy-based vase back on the dresser. She felt incredibly stupid but relief quickly gave way to sheer fury and she glared at Rafe. 'You don't know how close you came to having this vase smashed over your head.'

From her tone Rafe surmised that she wished she'd carried out the planned attack. Her cheeks were flushed, her hair a tumble of gold silk on her shoulders and despite her voluminous pyjamas he was swamped with a mixture of desire and tenderness as he studied her furious face.

'You seem to be making a habit of walking into my home

uninvited,' she snapped. 'How did you get in? Don't tell me the front door was open because I know I locked it.'

In reply, he dangled his door key in front of her and she stared at it, her puzzlement obvious. 'Actually, it's my home,' he corrected mildly and she drew a sharp breath.

'Since when was your name Hank Molloy?'

'Hank is the chief executive of a subsidiary company of the Santini Corporation who arranged the lease of this house. I understand you're my housekeeper—welcome on board.'

Sneaky didn't cover it; Machiavellian was nearer the mark. She'd known there had to be a catch and patently he was it. He was studying her with indolent amusement, all powerful, dominant male, his black jeans and leather jacket emphasising his height and raw sexual magnetism, and it took all her reserves of willpower to resist his pull.

'I assume you have a good reason for what is almost certainly a fraudulent act—tricking me into signing that contract,' she qualified, and he gave a slow smile.

'Several.'

'Do you care to explain them?'

'A practical demonstration would be more illuminating.' He closed the space between them in a heartbeat, his hand cupping her nape to angle her head so that he could plunder her mouth at will. Resistance was impossible when her senses were drugged by the seductive musk of his cologne. The heat from his body enfolded her, his arms drawing her in against the solid wall of his chest and she could feel his heart thudding furiously beneath her fingertips. He kissed her until her lips were swollen, until she was boneless and totally pliant in his arms, and only then did he ease back a fraction, brushing his mouth gently over hers while she clung to him, desperate to prolong the moment before she would have to admit that her defences had crumbled at the first attack.

'Why are you hounding me?' she whispered when he released her and she wrapped her arms defensively around her body. 'What do you want from me?'

The answer was simple but she wasn't ready to hear it, he acknowledged grimly, her air of vulnerability and the tremulous quiver of her lips causing him a momentary attack of conscience. Perhaps he should let her go, walk away and forget the closeness they'd once shared, the *joy*, but he'd tried keeping his distance and four years on she still dogged his every waking thought.

'I'm hardly hounding you, *cara mia*; you're in my house, sleeping in my bed—figuratively speaking, that is,' he added when she looked as though she would explode.

'Do you honestly expect me to believe that my position here as housekeeper is sheer coincidence?' she demanded bitingly, and he shrugged.

'Hell, no; it took a lot of planning and I still couldn't be certain that when your eager estate-agent friend was asked to find a suitable housekeeper at short notice he would appoint you. He might just have easily given the position to his elderly receptionist, and I have to admit I wouldn't have greeted her so enthusiastically.'

His eyes glinted with amusement as he studied her flushed face and she was torn between the desire to hit him and to burst into tears. She'd forgotten how he loved to tease her, forgotten his easy sense of humour and the laughter they'd shared, and she didn't want to remember any of it now.

'I'm sure Gloria will be an excellent replacement,' she told him coolly, 'because I have no intention of staying here with you.' Swiftly, she ran from the room, tore up the stairs to her bedroom and pulled her suitcase from under the bed. She was in the process of piling her clothes into it when he appeared in the doorway, but she ignored him, her movements jerky and uncoordinated as she tried to fasten the zip.

'You know it's raining?' he queried mildly.

'I don't care.' The storm had worked itself up to a crescendo, the rain smashing against the window. 'I'd sooner go out in a hurricane than spend one more minute under the same roof as you.' He was blocking the doorway, an immovable force, but she pushed against his chest anyways, needing to get away from him before she did something stupid like beg him to kiss her again. 'What part of "I don't want to give our relationship another chance" do you not understand?' she shouted, but even that didn't provoke the loss of temper she was expecting.

'This part,' he said softly, and this time his lips were gentle, his kiss so full of tender compassion that the tears behind her eyelids escaped and slid down her cheeks. He had cupped her face with both his hands and stilled fractionally when he felt wetness on his fingers, but he didn't lift his head, just deepened the kiss, coaxing a response she was powerless to deny.

When he'd done she stepped back, her eyes dark with a mixture of desire and confusion. How could one kiss evoke such a stark hunger for more and, God damn it, what had happened to her *pride*? 'Let me go,' she pleaded huskily but he merely smiled.

'I'm the one who's going. I fly to Canada tomorrow and after the Grand Prix I'm returning to Italy and then on to Bahrain. You signed a contract that stipulated you would give three months' notice should you want to leave,' he reminded her. 'At the weekend one of my top executives arrives in Oxford to oversee the takeover of the factory the Santini Corporation recently bought out. Bruno and his wife and four children are looking forward to staying in an English country house, especially as they've been assured that a resident housekeeper will be on hand to assist them.'

His tone was amiable but Eden sensed the steel resolve behind his words and her fingers tightened around the handle of her suitcase. 'Nev will find someone else to look after the Dower House,' she argued. 'I refuse to be manipulated by you, Rafe. You might have been able to boss me around before but the spell's broken; I'm not in awe of you any more and I won't jump to your bidding whenever you click your fingers.'

'But you have nowhere else to go,' he pointed out, his jaw rigid, and she could see he was fighting to control his temper.

'I'll find a flat. If the other one hadn't fallen through at the last minute I wouldn't be here now.' She paused as an incredible thought struck her. 'The flat on the Cob Tree estate—you couldn't have… Tell me you didn't…?' A couple of hundred thousand pounds was loose change to him but surely he hadn't bought the flat to prevent her from renting it?

'It's a nice little investment,' he admitted idly, 'although the location isn't great.'

'You bastard, Rafe, I won't let you do this to me. I don't even know why you're bothering. Is it some misplaced desire to get your own back, to punish me for a sin I didn't commit?'

He towered over her, the hard planes of his face and the rigid stance of his body faintly menacing. He was used to having his own way and hated to be thwarted. 'I believe that what we had, what we could have again, is worth fighting for,' he told her fiercely, 'and I don't care if I have to play dirty to get what I want.'

'Which is what, precisely?'

'You, back in my bed, where you belong.'

For one crazy moment she hovered on a pinnacle of indecision as capitulation beckoned, and then the mist cleared and she shook her head.

'I don't belong to you, Rafe. You set me free a long time ago and I have no intention of coming back.'

CHAPTER FOUR

THE aroma of freshly ground coffee drifting from the kitchen warned Eden that her unwelcome visitor was still in residence. Having vowed that she wouldn't sleep a wink while under the same roof as Rafe, she'd been horrified to find her room bathed in sunshine when she woke up, a disbelieving glance at her watch revealing that it was almost ten o'clock.

'*Buon giorno, cara,*' he greeted idly, lowering his newspaper fractionally to survey her, and Eden closed her eyes as a wave of memories rolled over her. She'd loved the intimacy of sharing breakfast with him in the big, cool kitchen of his villa that nestled on the edge of Lake Como. Despite his fabulous wealth he was a man of simple tastes, simple pleasures. He employed few staff at the villa and more than anything she'd loved the fact that they were able to spend time alone, away from the circus of the Formula 1 scene. Energetic nights followed by lazy days had been a way of life for a few precious weeks and she had treasured the closeness they shared.

How had it fallen apart so spectacularly? she wondered despairingly. How could he have been so taken in by Gianni's lies? The painful answer was that he hadn't trusted her. To him she had been just another in a long line of women who briefly shared his life and bed, and when it came to crunch time, family loyalty, the blood ties that bound him so closely to the Santinis, had won over a relationship that meant little to him.

'I thought you were leaving,' she snapped, desperate to disguise the way her heart flipped at the sight of him sitting at the table, and his brows rose quizzically.

'You were never this grouchy when you used to spend the night in my bed, but sexual frustration is a well-known cause of depression. Want me to cheer you up?' he added unforgivably and she glared at him.

'The only thing that'll cheer me up is the sight of you walking out of the door, with the assurance that you won't be coming back.' She boiled the kettle and reached into a cupboard for the garish green teapot that was shaped like a frog.

'I see you still have a fascination for slimy creatures,' he observed and she stared at him pointedly.

'I wouldn't bank on it, I stopped being fascinated by you a long time ago.'

His low chuckle did strange things to her equilibrium, as did the slow smile that curved his mouth.

'I assure you I'm not slimy, *cara mia*. Touch me and see.' He moved before she had time to react and she gave an indignant yelp as he jerked her onto his lap, her frantic wriggling to escape only ceasing when she discovered the effect it was having on a certain area of his anatomy.

'You're disgusting,' she hissed, temper her only weapon

against the warmth that flooded through her, as she was held captive against his thighs. 'Let me up, Rafe, you've proved your point—you're not in the least bit slimy and neither, actually, are frogs,' she added, desperate to take her mind off the throbbing hardness of his arousal she could feel beneath her bottom. 'They're cute and definitely my favourite animal.'

'Which presumably is why, when everyone else presented me with expensive gifts after winning the world championship for the fourth time, you gave me a green plastic frog that squeaked.'

Rafe watched the soft colour stain her cheeks with an element of satisfaction. When he had first seen her at the Press conference he'd been struck by her new air of sophistication, but this morning, in her faded jeans and cotton T-shirt, her hair a tangle of gold silk around her sleep-flushed face, she looked like the young, innocent Eden who haunted his dreams. She wasn't as sure of herself as she would have him believe, or as immune to the sexual chemistry that fizzed between them.

With a determined effort she slid off his lap, and the fresh, lemony scent of her hair evoked a curious pain in his chest. Indigestion, he told himself derisively as he glanced down at his paper, but the printed page meant nothing and when he looked at her again the pain was still there.

'I guess the plastic frog was a pretty stupid gift,' she muttered, 'but I didn't know what else to buy for a man who had everything.'

He hadn't had the one thing he really wanted, Rafe reflected and he wondered what she would say if he told her he competed in every race with a squeaky amphibian squashed into the pocket of his flame suit.

'When are you going,' she demanded, 'and, more to the point, when is your executive and his family due to arrive? It would be nice to have a bit of notice, something you obviously didn't feel was necessary.'

'I phoned several times yesterday evening to inform you I was on my way to Wellworth,' Rafe told her coolly. 'You must have been busy, or out somewhere.'

His questioning tone irritated her. What right did he have to query her every move? 'I had dinner with Nev,' she informed him sweetly. 'We didn't get back until late.'

'You entertained him here? Not a wise move, *cara*; don't do it again.'

'Excuse me! What right do you have to veto my friends? And I didn't *entertain* Nev in the way you're suggesting, I simply made him a cup of coffee. It seems ridiculous in the light of things now, but I wanted to thank him for giving me the opportunity to live in the Dower House. If I'd known you were involved I wouldn't have bothered.'

'Just make sure you're not tempted to thank him too enthusiastically,' Rafe warned darkly, and her temper caught fire.

'I'll do what I like and you can go to hell,' she bit out, shaking back her hair and glaring at him, her hands on her hips.

'Not in my house, *cara mia*, and not at all if you value your life.'

He was the most arrogant, infuriating man she had ever met and she felt like stamping her foot like a child in the throes of a temper tantrum. 'Fine, I quit. I'll move my stuff out of the house today and you can find another damn housekeeper to run around your executives.'

'You signed a contract.'

'Which wouldn't stand up in court,' she challenged.

He shrugged nonchalantly. 'Possibly not, although I'm prepared to test its legality. More pertinently, word going round that your friend Monkton can't be relied upon to hire suitable staff would be highly damaging to his business. He deals with a lot of exclusive country-house lets, doesn't he?'

'I hate you,' Eden flung at him bitterly when she realised she had run out of retorts. 'You can't stand not having your own way, can you?'

'I pursue what I want with single-minded determination,' he corrected her, 'and I always win. You should know that by now, *cara.*' He folded his newspaper and closed the lid of his briefcase before he spared her a glance, seemingly unmoved by her bristling fury. 'Bruno is due to arrive on Tuesday. He's aware that you work for the newspaper during the day and you're not expected to run around like a skivvy. However, I assume you'll get up earlier in the mornings, and you'll have to tidy yourself up a bit.'

Eden took a deep breath and counted to ten as his gaze roamed her admittedly dishevelled appearance. She'd dressed in a hurry and simply grabbed the first items of clothing on the top of her suitcase. Her jeans were faded and paint-spattered and her T-shirt had shrunk in the wash so that it clung to her body, drawing attention to the fact that she wasn't wearing a bra. The atmosphere in the kitchen was suddenly sizzling with electricity as Rafe focused on her breasts, and to her shame she felt them swell and tighten.

'Are you cold, *cara*?' he queried mockingly and she blushed and folded her arms across her chest in an effort to hide the prominent peaks of her nipples. It didn't help that he was impeccably dressed. His grey suit was superbly tailored, no doubt designer, as were his silk shirt and tie, and today he looked like the powerful head of a global company rather than a racing driver, but of course, now that his father was unwell, he had to fill both roles.

'Let's make a deal. I'll go and change into something more suitable and you'll just…go!'

His laughter followed her up the stairs, and his query, 'When did you develop that sassy tongue?' didn't deserve an answer, although she took a savage satisfaction in slamming her bedroom door.

The house was empty when she went back downstairs and she assured herself she was glad. It was time to look to the future and Rafe didn't feature in hers. She dumped her suitcase in the hall and groaned as she remembered she had left her bedroom window open. Although she had no intention of staying in the Dower House, she didn't want to be held responsible if it were burgled. Besides, she already loved this house and couldn't bear the idea of it being ransacked by intruders.

She'd known that the chance to live here in its gentle splendour was too good to be true, she thought dismally as she took one last look round, but as she was about to lock the French doors that led onto the terrace a movement caught her eye. Rafe was standing by the fish pond, his arms folded across his chest, his stance as arrogant and supremely self-confident as ever until she looked more closely. He was unaware of her presence and she was able to study him, her greedy eyes travelling over him, drinking him in.

He looked older, she realised with a pang. It was four years, after all, and his life on the racing circuit was demanding, both physically and emotionally. She remembered the intense pressure he had been under to win every race. As a young man his father, Fabrizzio, had been a brilliant engineer whose marriage to the daughter of a wealthy car manufacturer had enabled him to develop the exclusive sports cars that had become one of Italy's major exports. Santini had already been a dynamic and successful company, but when Rafe won his first world championship driving the car that had been developed exclusively by his father's company, it rocketed the Santini name to the top of the table alongside other world leaders such as Ferrari and Renault. The pride and fortune of the Santini Corporation, of Italy itself, it seemed, rested on the shoulders of the country's golden boy. Rafe was a national hero but the price of such adulation was high and the idea of failure inconceivable.

It was lonely at the top, he once confided, and she had looked around the packed room at the throng of guests who had come to celebrate another win, and laughed. At the time she had thought he was joking—everyone wanted to be with Rafe, everyone wanted a piece of him, so how on earth could he be lonely? Watching him now, she suddenly understood and with that understanding came remorse and shame, because she had been as guilty as any of demanding her share of him.

Suddenly he looked up and trapped her gaze, but instead of feeling embarrassed that she had been caught staring at him she was shocked at the bleakness in his dark eyes before his lashes fell, concealing his expression.

'Why did you think I was going to marry Valentina?' he asked quietly and Eden shrugged and tore her eyes from him to stare at a patch of daises.

'Gianni told me.'

'Gianni!' Rafe's head came up and there was no disguising the shock in his eyes. 'I don't believe you.'

'It's the truth,' she insisted. 'The night you found us together by the pool, it wasn't what you thought. Gianni had just explained that an arrangement between the Santini and de Domenici families had been made years before, and you were determined to marry Valentina to please Fabrizzio.'

'I am not my father's puppet,' Rafe bit out furiously, 'and this is the twenty-first century; arranged marriages went out several hundred years ago.'

'Do you deny that you ever discussed marriage to her with Fabrizzio?'

'It was mentioned,' Rafe admitted with a shrug. 'My father would have liked it, it's true, but he knew there was no chance of it happening.'

'But Gianni told me,' Eden cried desperately. This was the first time Rafe had ever really listened to her, but the contemptuous disbelief in his eyes made it hard to go on. 'He said the fact that you seemed to delight in making our affair so very public, the newspaper scoops and the magazine articles about our relationship, was a ploy. You knew that when you appeared to end our affair, it would be headline news that would please Valentina and her family. But if you believed I would have stayed as your mistress after your marriage, you really didn't know me at all.'

Rafe's jaw tightened ominously but his voice was deceptively soft as he queried, 'And Gianni told you this? My brother, who is dead and cannot defend himself? Now, that's what I call convenient.'

'Why would I lie?' Eden demanded angrily. 'Gianni didn't want to tell me, but things hadn't been right between us for weeks. You were cold and distant and I suspected that you'd grown tired of me. I badgered Gianni until he admitted what you were planning and when you found us together he was comforting me, that's all—despite what he said about us having a secret affair.'

'So that's your version of the truth?' he drawled sardonically, and the tiny flicker of hope in her chest drowned in the depths of his scornful expression. 'Is that really the best you can come up with, *cara*?'

'The truth,' Eden stated with deadly calm, 'is that you are a deceitful, two-timing bastard who hoped to increase his social standing by marrying the daughter of an aristocrat whilst having a mistress conveniently tucked away in the background. This is hopeless,' she muttered. 'You made your mind up about me four years ago and you still haven't got the guts to admit you might have been wrong.'

'I *saw* you, and not just that night. You always had your eyes on Gianni, you were always laughing with him.'

'He was the only one of your family who was nice to me,' Eden said, defending herself. 'Your father made it obvious that he despised me and everyone else followed his lead and treated me like I had bubonic plague. I only had eyes for you,' she whispered sadly, and she still had. He was the only man she had ever loved, the reason, if she was honest, why she had spent the last three years living in constant danger. Focusing on her survival had been the only way she could prevent herself from thinking about him and the life they had once shared.

He, on the other hand, had spent the years since they'd parted jetting around the world, spending his time in glamorous locations with equally glamorous women. She was all too aware that he possessed a high sex drive. Add to that his stunning looks and plenty of Latin charm and it was impossible to believe he had spent the time pining for her.

'How you have the nerve to accuse me of cheating on you beats me when not a week goes by without a feature in the tabloids about you and your latest conquest,' she said bitterly, tensing as he walked around the pool towards her.

'I've had other lovers in the last four years, I can't deny it,' he told her with a shrug, and Eden felt a knife skewer her heart at his casual admission. 'As you say, there are plenty of women on the circuit who advertise their availability, and I have never pretended to be a monk,' he went on, ruthlessly ignoring the flare of pain in her eyes. 'But while we were together I was faithful to you. I certainly wasn't eyeing up members of your family.'

She had to get away from him before her composure cracked. Already she could feel the ache of tears behind her eyelids and she spun away, stumbling blindly towards the steps leading to the house.

'The other women, they meant nothing,' Rafe insisted, catching hold of her shoulder and forcing her to turn and face him. 'I used to close my eyes and pretend I was with you.'

'That's sick,' Eden whispered, and watched, wide-eyed, as he lowered his head until his mouth was millimetres from her own.

'It's the truth,' he whispered back before his lips claimed hers in a kiss that drove every other thought but him from her mind.

Her first instinct was to resist, and it was a desperate attempt at self-preservation that had her beating her fists against his shoulders as she fought the insidious warmth that flooded through her. In reply, he merely tightened his grip and hauled her up close against his chest while his hand at her nape angled her head so that there was no escape from his mouth, which seemed intent on taking everything she was so unwilling to give. His tongue traced the outline of her lips and she clamped them shut, refusing him access as his careless admission that he had had other lovers taunted her.

The image of him holding another woman in his arms, of him kissing her, caressing her, making love to her, caused her body to clench in rejection. It was unbearable and she *hated* him but at the same time it was growing harder and harder to fight her response to the mastery of his touch. He knew her so well, too well, even after all this time, and her fists slowly unfurled and crept up around his neck, the feel of silky black hair between her fingers evoking memories of how he had loved her to massage his shoulders after a race. The pressure of his lips increased and suddenly she couldn't fight him any more. Her mouth parted on a little gasp as he slid his hand down to her bottom, forcing her thighs up against the hardness of his, his arousal a potent force that made her realise she wasn't the only one who was spinning out of control.

'I have fantasised about making love to you every night for the past four years,' he admitted huskily when at last he lifted his head, but by then she was beyond any sort of reply.

Her lips were bruised and stinging and as she ran her tongue over them his eyes narrowed and he muttered something in Italian before he swept her into his arms. As he laid her down, the coolness of the grass broke through the sensual haze that surrounded her, but when she struggled to sit up he came down on top of her, the weight of him crushing her into the earth. Overhead, the leaves on the trees formed an intricate lace canopy beyond which she could see the sky, cloudless and an intense blue. The sweet smell of the grass mingled with the scent of his cologne, musky, male and fiercely elemental, and her senses quivered in recognition of the only man who had ever been a part of her. His mouth captured hers again, gentler this time, as if he knew he had breached her defences, but no less passionate, the sweep of his tongue hot and hungry, fanning the flames of her desire.

His fingers moved to the hem of her T-shirt, his eyes darkening as he pushed it up to reveal her breasts. 'The fantasy was never this good,' he repeated thickly, and she trembled, her body on fire as he lowered his head. She arched up to meet him, unable to stifle her groan of pleasure when he stroked his tongue over her taut nipple. The caress was light, teasing her, tormenting her, and she dug her nails into his shoulders until his mouth closed fully around the throbbing peak and he suckled her. A shaft of sensation coiled through her, so intense that she held him tighter and arched her hips as he rocked between her thighs in an erotic simulation of making love to her.

It was only when she felt his hands release the button at the waistband of her jeans, felt him slide the zip down ready to ease the denim over her hips, that reality hit and with it the realisation that if Rafe removed her jeans he would see her scarred leg. What was she *doing*? Was she completely mad? He believed her to be a liar and a cheat. His opinion of her couldn't get any lower, yet she was about to offer him a quickie on the grass before he flew off to the other side of the world.

Feeling the sudden tension that gripped her body, he stilled, watching her with hooded eyes as she frantically sought to push his hands away.

'No, I don't want this,' she told him fiercely, and he gave a harsh laugh as he rolled off her and lay on his back to stare up at the sky.

'So I noticed, *cara*. I wonder if you know what you do want,' he drawled, cold fury in his eyes as he watched her tug her T-shirt down and scramble to her feet.

'Not you, that's for sure.'

'Is that the reason you're running away? I tripped over your suitcase in the hall,' he added, and she blushed.

'I thought you'd already left.'

'And were you waiting until then to sneak off?'

'I wasn't sneaking anywhere,' she snapped. 'You must see that I can't stay here.'

He rolled onto his side, his head supported on his arm as he studied her silently.

'And if I asked you to stay?'

'Give me one good reason why I should.'

'Another chance at a relationship neither of us can dismiss or deny,' he suggested quietly, and she shook her head, refusing to listen to her heart.

'We've been there, discussed that and I refuse to enter a

relationship with a man who doesn't trust me. I have never lied to you,' she stated with such intensity that the hand around his heart squeezed tight.

'Which means that Gianni—my little brother, who I trusted with my life—did,' he murmured, with a depth of emotion in his voice that crucified her. 'I didn't cause his crash,' he said quietly as he slowly got to his feet, and she put her hand on his arm, desperate to comfort him. He looked *crushed*, there was no other word for it, and she ached for him, the lonely years apart and the bitterness suddenly immaterial.

'I know you didn't,' she assured him, but he didn't seem to hear her, lost in his thoughts.

'I loved him, and the intense rivalry between us was never as serious as everyone else believed, or so I thought. At the Hungarian Grand Prix, I realised just how serious it had become. Gianni was desperate to beat me and I could have let him pass, should have done. Instead, he took a stupid risk, hit the bend too fast, and I will never forget watching his car spin off the track.' He walked slowly into the house, his back rigid, and Eden hurried after him. 'That night, sitting in Intensive Care watching him wired up to all those machines, I promised myself that nothing would come between us again, and that I would end the row that had split us.'

'What did you row about?' she whispered, her heart thudding fearfully as she anticipated his reply. 'Was it about me?' His silent nod confirmed the worst and she blinked back her tears. 'No wonder you hate me. Gianni's accident was my fault.'

'Gianni's accident was Gianni's fault,' he told her firmly.

'It's taken me three years to realise that. He took an unneces-sary risk and paid the price, but watching him struggle to come to terms with his paralysis was hard. I felt guilty that I had everything and he had nothing. Losing you was a private hell, but it was nothing compared to the torment he was going through, and in the end I couldn't save him. He chose to end his life.'

For the first time Eden understood how agonising the last few years must have been for Rafe. It must have been a shock to find her in Gianni's arms, and perhaps it was understand-able that he'd initially believed his brother over her, she admitted honestly. She had been too hurt to try and defend herself, and by the time Rafe's temper had cooled enough for him to maybe listen to her, Gianni had crashed and been left with his terrible injuries. Rafe had been unable to help him. All he could do was give him his support and trust.

'I have to go—my jet's waiting for me,' he muttered as he strode through the house, stopping only to collect his brief-case and slide his arms into his jacket. 'Where will you go? To Neville Monkton?'

'No! There's nothing going on between us. I don't know what I'm going to do,' Eden admitted huskily. She didn't know what to think, how to react to everything he'd told her, but there was no time to discuss things further; he was already heading out the front door.

He slung his case onto the back shelf of the sports car before coiling his long frame behind the wheel. He'd said he had to leave but he seemed to be taking an inordinately long time to get going, and as she watched him fiddle with the controls on the dashboard she had the strange feeling that he was reluctant to start the engine. Eventually it fired, the throaty roar reminding her of the times she'd stood at the trackside while the cars hurtled past at terrifying speeds, and she was gripped with apprehension.

'Rafe!' He was already turning out of the drive, but he must have seen her in the mirror and he hit the brakes before opening the window.

'What's wrong, *cara*?'

He was so gorgeous, his face all hard planes and satiny olive skin, his black hair gleaming in the sunlight, but she focused on his mouth, remembering the sweetness of his kiss.

'Be careful,' she whispered, leaning down so that her face was on level with his, and his slow smile took her breath away.

'I'll promise to be careful if you'll promise to stay.' He gave her no chance to reply, but slid his hand into her hair to pull her against the car, his lips taking possession of hers with a tenderness that brought tears to her eyes. He increased the pressure slightly, coaxing her response, and she closed her eyes and gave in to pure sensation. 'Do we have a deal?'

She was beyond words and could only stare at him, unaware of the wealth of emotions in her eyes, the confusion. There was still a long way to go, he conceded silently, but it was a journey he was determined to take.

CHAPTER FIVE

'ALL things considered, you've made a pretty remarkable recovery,' the surgeon told Eden as he studied the X-rays of her injured leg. 'The metal pins will stay a permanent feature, I'm afraid—they're what's holding the shattered bone together—but it's all knitting together nicely and I see the scars are fading.'

Privately, Eden couldn't see much improvement to the purple welts that ran the length of her shin, but Dr Hillier was so enthusiastic about her recovery that she felt she couldn't complain. The simple truth was that she was lucky to be alive, and having met countless victims of land-mine explosions while she was in Africa, many of whom had lost limbs, she felt a few scars were nothing.

'If you pop behind the screen and put your clothes on, I'll ask the nurse to make an appointment for six months' time.' Dr. Hillier frowned at the noise of raised voices outside the door. 'Sounds like another satisfied National Health customer,' he murmured as the nurse on the reception desk cried, 'You can't just barge in…'

'Now, look here,' Eden heard the eminent surgeon at the

London hospital say firmly. 'Good God! Rafael Santini—
what are you doing here?'

Good question, Eden thought as she scrambled frantically
into her clothes. A furtive peep from behind the screen had
revealed that Rafe was very much here, big and dark and,
from the look of it, in a raging temper.

'Eden, where are you? What are you doing?' he demanded
as she stepped from behind the screen, and her heart flipped
painfully in her chest at the sight of him after two weeks apart.

'Getting dressed,' she told him calmly, and he took a deep
breath, his nostrils flaring as his gaze swung from her to the
hapless doctor.

'You mean you stripped off in front of *him*?' Rafe was on
a roll, black eyes flashing fire, his fists clenched, and Dr
Hillier backed up against his desk.

'A nurse was present. It's all quite above board, I assure
you,' he murmured nervously.

'Dr. Hillier is the surgeon who operated on my leg,' Eden
explained, giving Rafe a fulminating glare. 'I don't know
what right you think you've got to storm in here. How did
you know where I was, anyways?'

With another furious glance at the surgeon, Rafe followed
her out of the consulting room. 'Your estate-agent friend told
me you had a hospital appointment. I arrived at the Dower
House to find it deserted,' he added accusingly. 'I knew Bruno
and his family had already gone back to Milan, but I
expected…hoped,' he amended, 'you would be there.'

They were incurring a lot of interest in the small waiting
area—hardly surprising, when Rafe seemed to fill the room—
and she sighed impatiently.

'Will you keep your voice down? You weren't due back until tomorrow night and even if I'd known you were coming early I couldn't have changed the appointment—it was made ages ago.'

'What's the matter with you?' His dark eyes trawled her from head to toe, oblivious to the curious onlookers.

'What do you mean? Nothing's the matter with me, other than annoyance at you barging into the consulting room. It was rude.'

Rafe muttered something that she suspected was extremely rude, in his native tongue. 'Why are you here, why did you need to see a doctor and what is the matter with your leg?' he asked with exaggerated patience, as if he were speaking to a halfwit.

She'd missed him so much, Eden acknowledged. She'd almost forgotten what it was like to feel this alive, yet five minutes in his company and the blood was zinging in her veins, as amusement and irritation filled her in equal measures. 'I hurt my leg while I was working in Africa,' she explained, but he remained standing in the middle of the room, blocking everyone's path as he waited for more. 'In an accident,' she added, and his frown deepened.

'A car accident?'

'No,' she hesitated briefly before murmuring, 'an explosion. I stepped on a land-mine—well, not completely on it, of course, or I wouldn't be here now, but something triggered it while I was standing a couple of feet away and…and I nearly lost my leg,' she finished quietly. Rafe looked as if he was going to explode himself, but then he suddenly swung round and flung open the door to the consulting room.

'And you say this doctor operated on your leg? I want to see him and I want a full explanation of the injuries you received.'

'Rafe, you can't just walk in there—he's a busy man, and there's an appointment system.' She was already talking to the back of his head and as he shut the door firmly behind him, she glanced helplessly at the nurse on the reception desk. 'I'm sorry, he's awful, isn't he?'

'I think he's rather wonderful,' the superior-looking nurse said with a grin that made her suddenly human. 'He's very dominant, isn't he?'

'You wouldn't believe,' Eden muttered. Without Rafe to entertain them, the small crowd in the waiting room turned their attention expectantly to her, and she hastily shot into the corridor and headed for the drinks machine.

When she returned ten minutes later she found Rafe leaning against the reception desk. The hospital was warm and she felt decidedly hot and bothered, but he looked cool and relaxed, and, in jeans and a black leather jacket, drop-dead gorgeous. The group of nurses around him obviously thought so, too, she noted sourly. He must be the only man capable of flirting with five women simultaneously, but as she approached he straightened up and strolled towards her.

'Ready to go?' he queried.

'I am—are you sure you can tear yourself away?'

His smile took her breath away and before she could recover, he cupped her chin and took her mouth in a deep, languorous kiss that instantly breached her defences. She was in shock, she defended herself as her lips parted beneath the gentle pressure of his. His mouth was warm and soft and infinitely inviting, and her eyelids drifted down as she lost herself in pure sensation.

'Let's go, *cara*. We're causing a scene.'

'Not we—you. I can't believe you did that.'

'Kissed you?' he asked innocently, and she glared at him as she marched along the corridor.

'I can't believe you stormed into Dr Hillier's room, twice! Heaven knows what he thought.'

'He was extremely helpful. He even showed me the X-rays of your leg after I told him I had your permission.'

'But you didn't!' She broke off with an impatient sigh. 'Rafe, why are you here?'

'Why didn't you tell me you'd been hurt?' Suddenly, he was intensely serious, his dark eyes scanning her delicate features as if trying to reassure himself that she was as fully recovered as the doctor had insisted.

Eden shrugged, wishing the husky concern in his voice didn't make her feel so emotional. Her leg was healing well, better than she'd expected, and she didn't need to relive memories of the explosion that still gave her nightmares.

'My welfare has nothing to do with you. You made that clear four years ago.'

Rafe bit back an oath. 'You could have died. The doctor said you lost so much blood it was touch and go for a while.'

'Well, I didn't. I'm here and I'm perfectly all right, so you can stop the sudden bout of concern.'

She was far from *all right*, he thought grimly. The X-rays might prove that her leg was healing, but the mental scars she'd incurred still haunted her. He could see the shadows in her eyes, and, from the brief description the doctor had given him of the explosion and the full extent of the injuries she'd received, he wasn't surprised. He was still fighting the wave of nausea that had swept over him when he pictured her bloodied and battered body, the guilt that he hadn't been there to save her. If he had believed her over Gianni, she would never have gone to Africa in the first place, never been so horrifically injured. But Gianni was his brother, his flesh and blood. Why would he have lied? It didn't make any sense.

'If you're OK, why are you limping?' he demanded as they reached the hospital exit.

'My leg aches a bit today, but it's hardly surprising when it's been prodded and poked all morning. I'll rest it on the train,' she added, and he frowned.

'Naturally I will drive you back to Wellworth. Did you really expect me to just drop you at the station?'

'I didn't expect to see you here at all,' Eden muttered. She could see his car parked on a double yellow line, but as they walked along the busy London street she was aware that they were the subject of speculative glances from every passer-by. It was to be expected, she supposed; he was six feet, four inches of olive-skinned perfection, and he would draw a second look even before it was realised that he was Formula 1's most famous competitor.

'I thought we could do some shopping while we're in town, but maybe it's not a good idea. Your leg is obviously painful.'

'It's fine, but shopping isn't,' she said firmly. 'You attract too much attention, Rafe, and I don't want a jaunt down Oxford Street to be snapped by the paparazzi. They'll say that we're back together again, which we're most definitely not.'

Rafe looked so stunned that she had actually refused him that she had to hide her smile. It had never happened four years ago, but she was determined he wouldn't walk all over her again.

'Is that better?' he demanded imperiously as he pulled a pair of designer shades out of his pocket and shoved them on his nose.

'Oh, yes, completely incognito. Now you look like a member of the Mafia.'

'Are you ashamed to be with me?'

'Of course not,' she denied, 'but I really don't want to go back to the days when I was featured in the tabloids as the latest addition to your stable.'

'No one ever thought of you like that,' he argued fiercely, and she laughed.

'The whole Santini team knew that my job as Press officer was a cover for the fact that I was your mistress, and if they didn't know, your father made sure they understood that I was your whore.'

He came to a halt by his car, retrieved the parking ticket from beneath the windscreen wiper and shoved it into his pocket without even glancing at it. 'I don't know how you can say something like that.'

'Fabrizzio called me it to my face,' she said stubbornly, and he glared at her, raking an impatient hand through his hair.

'I don't believe you. You're lying.'

'Here we go again,' she muttered wearily. 'Same old story. I'm not lying, Rafe. I've never lied to you, about Gianni or your father or anything else, but I'm sick of having to defend myself. Your father despised me. He wanted you to marry your fancy Italian aristocrat. Maybe he even set Gianni up to lie to me about her, I don't know.'

'Why the hell would he do that?' Rafe shouted, and she took a step back, anticipating the scene of all scenes played out on one of the most public thoroughfares in London.

'Because he wanted to split us up?' she suggested, and he threw back his head and let out a harsh laugh.

'Well, he needn't have bothered. You'd already decided that one Santini couldn't keep you satisfied, and were determined to have the pair. We split up because I caught you making love with Gianni.'

She really couldn't take any more. Already, tears were burning behind her eyelids, queuing up to fall, but she'd be damned if she would let him see her cry. 'Fine, you win. Believe what you like, you will anyways, but the reason we split up, Rafe, is that you had no faith in me, in the same way that I have absolutely no faith in you now, or ever will again.'

She started to walk swiftly away from him. Up ahead, a bus had pulled into the kerb and she broke into a run, jumping onto the platform just as it pulled away.

'Where to, love?' The conductor waited imperturbably while she mopped her cheeks with a tissue.

'King's Cross.'

'Not on this bus—you're going the wrong way; this goes to Marble Arch.'

She didn't care if it went to Timbuktu as long as it meant she was out of reach of Rafe, she thought miserably as she handed over her change and stared unseeingly out of the window.

'So where are we going? I thought you didn't want to be seen in public with me.'

Her eyes widened as Rafe slid onto the bench seat next to her. Heaven knew how he had caught the bus—he must have sprinted after it, but she was far from impressed.

'I don't,' she said pointedly, 'so go away.'

'Do you really think I'd let you wander around London, alone and upset?' he queried gently, and she quickly looked away before she drowned in the velvet softness of his eyes.

'I don't know, I haven't seen you for four years. Why are you suddenly acting like you care, especially as you're the reason I'm upset?'

'There's something between us…' he began, and she rounded on him fiercely.

'No, there isn't, Rafe, not any more. You threw it away when you believed everyone including the cat's mother, over me. I don't want to listen to your reasons,' she added when he made to speak. 'I don't want to talk about the past any more.'

'Good, then we can concentrate on the present,' he said coolly, and she swallowed at the determined gleam in his eyes. 'We'll start from the beginning and get to know one another like two ordinary people. Hi, I'm Rafe Santini; I'm a racing driver.'

Every head on the bus turned, and Eden shook her head, absolutely determined that she wouldn't smile.

'You could never be described as ordinary, Rafe,' she murmured as his big hand closed over hers.

'Nor could you, *cara*, nor could you,' he growled huskily.

He was still holding her hand when they got off the bus and wandered across to Hyde Park. She ought to pull free of his grasp and demand that he leave her alone, she thought, but the honest truth was that she wanted to be with him. She wished they could start from scratch as he had suggested, but there was too much mistrust on either side, emotions that were still too raw, and her only possible saviour, who might prove her innocence, had taken his secrets to his grave.

'How did you get on with Bruno and his family?' Rafe asked as they strolled along the edge of the Serpentine, which glistened like a wide silver ribbon beneath the summer sky.

'Great; he and his wife are a lovely couple, and the children are beautiful.'

For two weeks the Dower House had rung with the noisy exuberance of four small children, the cries and gurgling laughter of the utterly adorable baby, but now the Martinellis were on their way back to Italy. She had enjoyed their company, Eden mused. They had filled a void left by Rafe and were so friendly that she'd had little chance to mope, although missing him had been a constant, nagging ache in her chest.

Watching the young family had brought on a severe case of envy when she witnessed the obvious devotion Bruno felt for his wife and children. If things had been different, could that have been her and Rafe? she had wondered wistfully. At twenty-seven, her hormones were kicking in and when she'd held the Martinellis' baby, she had been overcome with longing for a child of her own.

She had no idea whether Rafe wanted children, they'd certainly never discussed the subject four years ago, and the fantasies she'd spun of marriage and a family had been a secret desire she'd never dared to voice. Rafe was a racing driver, she reminded herself impatiently, an international playboy whose first loves were speed and excitement. She couldn't imagine him ever settling down to a life of domestic bliss, and if he really was serious about giving their relationship another chance, she would have to accept that it would be on his terms, following the nomadic lifestyle that life as a Formula 1 driver demanded.

She must need her head tested if she was even considering going back to him, she thought grimly. She'd hated life in the public eye, their affair played out in the tabloids and glossy magazines. She wasn't a supermodel or glamorous actress, and the paparazzi had speculated constantly on who Rafe might decide to replace her with when he tired of her—which, they suggested, he surely must. Four years ago she'd been unsure of herself and her role in his life. How much worse would it be now, when he believed she had cheated on him with his brother? He said he wanted them to have another chance, but it would be impossible when a chasm of suspicion divided them, and she couldn't bear to have her heart broken again. It still hadn't properly recovered from the first time.

Even wearing his sunglasses, or possibly because of them, Rafe was still spectacularly recognisable and was stopped several times by excited fans who requested his autograph.

'I can't help it,' he muttered as she watched him scribble his name on the back of a stunning brunette's T-shirt. 'Formula 1 attracts a lot of interest, nowadays.'

'No, you attract a lot of interest.' It was ridiculous to feel so jealous; she didn't even care any more, she reminded herself irritably.

'This is hopeless, I can't talk to you when you're in this mood.' He glanced along the lake to the little hut that hired out rowing boats. 'Come on, we surely can't be disturbed in the middle of the water, unless you object to the ducks.' He caught hold of her hand and dragged her after him, unmoved by her protests.

'I don't want to go in a boat. Take someone else. Heaven knows you've got enough choice of females who'd give their right arm to be stuck in the middle of the Serpentine with you.'

'*Madre de Dio*! You would try the patience of twenty saints.' He lifted her bodily into the rowing boat, shrugged out of his jacket and threw it at her with barely leashed violence. She'd opened her mouth to continue the argument, but the sight of him in his tight black T-shirt that clung like a second skin to the muscles of his abdomen rendered her speechless. He had an incredible body, she conceded as she tried to look anywhere but his powerful shoulders and the rippling of his biceps as he rowed them into the centre of the lake. Her mouth felt suddenly dry as she pictured him without the T-shirt, remembered the feel of him, skin on skin, his hair-roughened thighs pressing against the softness of hers.

The only man she had ever wanted; would ever want. Her life suddenly stretched ahead as a long and lonely road, but what was the alternative? To pick up the pieces of their affair and enjoy it while it lasted? She'd done it once, lived with the uncertainty that he would end it any day, soon. She didn't think she was strong enough to do it again.

It was surprisingly peaceful on the lake, and hard to believe they were in the middle of London. The noise of the traffic had receded to a distant hum and she tipped her head back and stared up at the sky.

'That's better,' Rafe noted in a satisfied tone. 'Relax, *cara*. It's not good to be so tense.'

'You make me tense,' she admitted with a sigh, and he gave her a wolfish grin.

'You make me tense, too, but I'm not complaining. Maybe we should help each other relax?'

She was powerless to resist when he turned on his seductive Latin charm. His voice curled around her like thick cream and she felt sleepy and supine, yet at the same time agonisingly aware of him. He had removed his sunglasses and she studied his face, his dark eyes beneath heavy black brows, the strong line of his nose and the sensual curve of his mouth. The feel of that mouth used to send her to heaven, she remembered, unable to drag her eyes from him, and he carefully drew the oars across the boat and leaned towards her.

'Do it,' he bade thickly, and she feigned confusion.

'Do what?'

'Kiss me. You know you want to.'

Pride dictated that she should refute the suggestion, but she felt boneless with longing and she had years ahead to work on restoring her pride. She hesitated fractionally, and then moved so that she was kneeling before him on the floor of the boat. She put one hand on his shoulder and drew his head down to hers, her mouth initiating a gentle exploration that speared his soul. He seemed content to let her control the kiss, taking only what she was willing to give, but he felt so good that the breath left her body in a rush as she increased the pressure, her tongue darting out to explore the contours of his lips.

Rafe hung on to his self-control with difficulty. She was

so beautiful, so warm and giving that he had to fight the urge to push her down onto the floor of the boat and make love to her there and then in broad daylight in the middle of a London park. Take it slow, his mind cautioned. One day at a time. There was too much hurt on both sides to rush things. The tentative probing of her tongue shattered that control, and he groaned and wrapped his arms around her, holding her close while the desire to assert his mastery became an overriding need. He deepened the kiss, passion overcoming his restraint, and he plundered the soft sweetness of her lips with a hunger that bordered on desperation.

She looked stunned when at last he released her and she sat back on her seat, her blue eyes dazed as she ran a shaky finger over her lips. Fool, she derided herself. She was falling into his honeyed trap, but dear God, it was the only place she wanted to be.

'How would you like to see the new musical that's just opened at the Palladium?' he asked as they walked back across the park.

'I'd love to, but it's been sold out for months.'

'I have tickets for tonight's performance, preceded by dinner at a particularly good restaurant I know.'

'I'm not dressed for the theatre,' Eden pointed out, and he shrugged.

'So we'll stop off and buy you something.'

'No.' The invitation to the show was too good to miss when it had received such excellent reviews, but that was all she would accept. 'I'll buy myself something to wear or I catch my train back to Wellworth.' Her arms were folded across her chest, her expression mutinous, and Rafe hid a smile. He didn't know where her fierce temper had sprung from—it certainly hadn't been evident during the year they'd spent together—but he possessed a fairly forceful personality, he admitted honestly. Had she been *afraid* of him? Surely not. The idea was all the more disturbing because he couldn't easily dismiss it. Patience wasn't his strong point and it was true he liked to have his own way, but his outbursts of temper, although explosive, were always short-lived. Perhaps he hadn't taken her feelings into account enough, he conceded. He'd been aware that she hated their life in the public eye, the intrusions into their private life by the tabloids. He had never courted the attention of the paparazzi, but he hadn't minded the pictures of the two of them. *Dio*, he'd been proud to show her off, to proclaim to the world that the beautiful little English rose was his woman, and maybe, if he was honest, it had been a way of getting the message across to his father, too.

'There's a problem you hadn't thought of,' Eden said with a frown as she emerged from the department store, clutching a carrier bag. She had dispatched Rafe to wait for her in the car after he had driven her mad by wandering around the shop, ostensibly trying to help. His selection of dresses with minuscule skirts had caused her a pang of despair. He wouldn't be quite so eager to see her in a skirt up to her eyebrows if he knew the state of her leg. 'Where am I going to get changed?' she queried worriedly, and he gave her a bland smile.

'At the hotel I've booked us into. I think of everything, *cara.*'

'Yes, well, you can just un-book us. I'm not sharing a room with you.'

'You really don't trust me, do you?' he murmured, an edge of seriousness in his voice as he deposited her bags in the back of the car, and Eden gave him a thoughtful look.

'No, I don't,' she said quietly. 'You let me down, Rafe, not the other way round, so don't even go there. Once I handed you my trust on a plate, but I won't be so careless again.'

They crawled through the London traffic in taut silence and Eden sighed as she rubbed her temples. Her head ached, her leg was throbbing and all she wanted to do was go home, except home—for now at least—was also Rafe's home, and whichever way she looked there didn't seem to be an escape route.

The hotel was one of London's finest, its opulence breathtaking, and she glanced around the suite they had been shown to with wide eyes. Rafe had stormed straight into the bedroom and she could hear the faint sounds of the shower from the *ensuite*. She could change into her dress in the sitting room, she supposed, but a shower was tempting, and was a safer way of relaxing than anything Rafe could suggest.

She almost turned tail at the sight of the king-sized bed, refusing to admit that she was filled with nervous excitement rather than trepidation at the idea of sharing it with him. The sensible option would be to slip out of the hotel, take a cab to the station and travel back to Wellworth, but she didn't feel sensible, she felt enervated, every nerve ending prickling with a sense of anticipation she couldn't deny, however hard she tried.

Rafe strolled out of the bathroom, a towel hitched around his waist, and her imagination immediately soared into overdrive at the thought of what was hidden beneath the towel. His hair was slicked to his head, droplets of water clinging to the black hairs that covered his chest, and she felt a curious sensation in the pit of her stomach, a need that was savage in its intensity, and darkened her eyes to the colour of cobalt.

'Do you want something, *cara*?' he queried coolly, and she felt her cheeks flame as she dragged her gaze from his glorious body.

'I, um…need to get changed,' she muttered, and his brows rose.

'Your room is at the opposite end of the sitting room, but I'm happy to share if you insist.'

'You could have said,' she snapped furiously, his sardonic smile telling her he was aware that she didn't just feel an idiot, she also felt agonisingly disappointed.

'You're so determined to think the worst of me, there didn't seem much point in wasting my breath, but let me make one thing clear, *cara*. I'm not so desperate that I need to try and trick you into my bed. I want you, sure,' he continued with a nonchalant shrug, as if the idea of making love to her was as important as choosing a sweet from the pick-and-mix counter, 'but I'm not going to take you kicking and screaming, so you can drop the air of maidenly outrage. One other thing,' he added, seeing that she was temporarily struck dumb. 'Stop looking at me like that with those big, hungry blue eyes.'

'Like what?' Eden managed through numb lips, and he gave her an insolent smile.

'Like you want me to throw you down on the bed and remove every last vestige of your clothing. Trail my lips all the way down your body and then spread those milky thighs I remember so well and thrust into you until we both reach the heights of sexual ecstasy.'

'I don't want you to do that,' she denied grittily, and his eyes narrowed. The tension between them was so intense, the imagery his words had evoked so stark, that one of them, surely, would have to crack.

'Which rather proves my point, *cara*,' he drawled softly. 'I still maintain you're a liar.'

CHAPTER SIX

THE dress was a peach-coloured, full-length sheath that emphasised her slender waist. The long skirt hid her legs while the strapless bodice revealed rather more of her full breasts than she was comfortable with. It was an overtly sexy dress and as Eden stood in front of the mirror she bitterly regretted the impulse that had led her to buy it, the secret hope that Rafe would find her attractive, despite the fact that the skirt hid her long limbs that he had always admired.

A sudden, unbidden image filled her mind, of him smoothing sunscreen over her stomach before trailing his hands lower, past the tiny triangle of material that masqueraded as a bikini, and down to her thighs. He was a leg man, he had informed her in his deep, sexy drawl, and she had laughed breathlessly and teased him by wrapping her long, tanned legs around him and holding him prisoner.

What would he make of her injuries? she wondered, and then shook her head impatiently. After his parting shot a couple of hours earlier, she doubted she would ever find out. He was never going to see her scarred leg. She was still smarting from the realisation that he was aware of her growing need for him, a desire that was becoming harder and harder to conceal. For his part, far from wanting to ravish her at the first opportunity, he seemed relaxed to the point of boredom, and his attitude of take it or leave it made her humiliation complete.

It was the reason she had remained locked in her bedroom, but she couldn't remain there forever. Pride—her only ally when her emotional stability seemed to have gone to pieces— dictated that she walk out and face him, and she checked her appearance one last time, sprayed a liberal amount of perfume on her wrists and opened the door.

Rafe swung round from the window, where he had been staring moodily down at the street, and felt his breath snag in his throat. Exquisite was the only word to describe her, and he felt a familiar ache in his loins as he took in the way her dress clung to her curves and her blonde hair was piled in a loose knot on top of her head. Sensual, sexy and right now as nervous as hell, he assessed, noting the way the pulse at the base of her throat was beating erratically. His woman, and despite the past, he was determined to reclaim her, but it wasn't proving quite as simple as he'd arrogantly assumed.

His gentle English rose had developed thorns, he conceded with a rueful smile. He could practically read the danger sign in her mind that warned him to keep away, but fortunately her body was throwing out different signals. The powerful sexual chemistry that had bound them together in the first place still burned. She didn't want to want him; he understood that and sympathised. He didn't enjoy being held at the mercy of his hormones, either, and it was only when he had accepted that desire was one of a multitude of intense emotions he felt for her that he'd been able to relax and bide his time.

'The dress was a good choice,' he said lightly, wanting to put her at her ease. But couldn't help adding huskily, 'You were always the most beautiful woman in the world to me.'

Eden took a shaky breath and closed her mind to the fact that he spent most of his life surrounded by exotic models. 'Thank you,' she replied quietly. 'Had you considered wearing glasses?'

His smile would melt an iceberg, she acknowledged with a sigh. She wanted to remain cool and aloof but it was difficult when he looked at her with such warmth in his dark eyes, and the bitter fury of a few hours ago seemed to have vanished.

'The car will be here in a minute to take us to the theatre. I thought we could eat afterwards, as the show has an early start. Are you happy with that, *cara*?'

She would be happy to stand here looking at him for the rest of the evening, but she could hardly say so. His black dinner suit emphasised the lean hardness of his body, and she wondered rather desperately if she should ask for a drink. A couple of glasses of wine might anaesthetise her reaction to him.

A discreet knock at the door heralded Room Service— champagne on ice with two glasses, and an exquisite bouquet of cream roses. Rafe handed them to her, selecting a single bloom that had been trimmed into a corsage.

'I thought you would like to wear a flower on your dress,' he murmured, his eyes glinting as he surveyed the creamy expanse of her naked shoulders. 'But there doesn't seem to be anywhere to pin it.'

He was too close, too vibrantly, excitingly alive, and

way too much for her to cope with, Eden thought despairingly as she took the flower from his grasp. 'It can go here, at the front,' she muttered, struggling to slide the pin into the low-cut bodice of her dress, and he moved closer still, taking the corsage from her nerveless fingers and attaching it so that the rose bud nestled in the valley between her breasts.

'Lucky flower,' he murmured teasingly, and she gave up all hope of acting cool. OK, so she fancied him, hungered for him, if she was honest. She knew it and so did he, and she would just have to deal with it, but at least while they were at the theatre she could drop her guard for a few hours and simply enjoy his company.

The show—a musical starring several internationally famous actors—was spectacular, and Eden enjoyed every minute of it. During dinner afterwards, Rafe entertained her with amusing stories from life on the racing circuit, and she rediscovered the man she had fallen in love with five years ago. He was witty and charming and seemed determined to steer the conversation away from the past, which suited Eden fine—she didn't want to think of anything but here and now. Yesterday was filled with disillusionment and pain, and tomorrow loomed an uncertain spectre, but now she had Rafe's undivided attention and she intended to make the most of it.

It was late when the limousine drew up outside the restaurant, and she was forced to admit she was glad they were spending the night at the hotel rather than travelling back to Wellworth. The soft leather seats of the Mercedes were inviting, and she closed her eyes for a moment that stretched to minutes, unaware that her head had settled on Rafe's shoulder. The voice in her ear was an intrusion, and she blinked as his face came into view, so close that she could see the fine lines at the corners of his eyes. Was this still part of her dream, or was it reality? she wondered. In her dream Rafe had lowered his head, the touch of his mouth as light as thistledown on hers, but had he kissed her or had she imagined it? She ran her tongue over her lips, trying to recapture the taste of him, and his eyes narrowed, a frown forming on his brow when he watched the way she tried to disguise her limp as she walked up the steps to the hotel entrance.

'You're tired, *cara*, it's been a long day for you. You must be desperate to climb into bed.'

Desperate to climb into his bed more like, a wicked voice in her head prompted, before every thought was banished from her mind as he swung her into his arms.

'Put me down—everyone's looking,' she demanded as she was forced to cling to his shoulders, and his low chuckle reverberated through his chest.

'The doorman and receptionist hardly make a packed audience. Your leg's hurting—don't even bother to deny it. You could barely walk up the steps. I blame myself,' he said grimly. 'I've overexerted you.'

He hadn't, but a list of the ways he *could* overexert her filled her wayward mind, and she sighed, fighting the urge to run her hand along his jaw and feel the faint stubble already evident, although he had shaved only a few hours before. He cradled her in his arms as the lift whisked them to the top floor and insisted on carrying her along the corridor to their suite, where he deposited her gently on the sofa.

'Do you think you can manage to get undressed?' he queried, his voice laced with concern, and Eden dropped her head as colour flooded her cheeks.

No, I need you to undress me, very slowly, answered the demon who had taken up residence in her head, and she gave herself a mental shake.

'I'll be fine,' she assured him brightly.

'Can I get you a nightcap?' He walked across to the bar and she couldn't drag her eyes from him, watching the way he moved with the lithe grace of an athlete. Now that he had discarded his jacket she could see the powerful muscle definition of his abdomen beneath his silk shirt and she ached to run her hands over him, feel his golden, satin skin beneath her fingertips and the brush of dark chest hair against her palms. He exuded a magnetism, a primitive sexual energy that tore through her barriers, and she closed her eyes for a few seconds, willing her self-control to reassert itself.

She didn't need any more alcohol, that was for sure. The champagne must have gone to her head and was the reason she felt hot and breathless. 'I think I'd better have coffee, strong and black, please. It might clear my head,' she added under her breath, and he gave her an assessing look.

'If you're worried I'm going to jump on you, don't be. I never pounce unless invited.'

He'd already made that clear earlier in the evening, she recalled miserably. It wasn't him she was worried about. He wasn't the one racked by desire and, if there was any pouncing to be done, she had a horrible feeling she would be the culprit.

'Actually, I think I'll just go to bed.' In her desperation to reach the sanctuary of her room, she stumbled and would have fallen but for the strong arms that caught her and lifted her into the air.

'Easy, there's no need to hurry,' he chided softly, but he didn't understand her urgency to break the spell he had cast over her and she wriggled frantically.

'I have to go to bed now,' she told him fiercely.

'Why?' His eyes narrowed as he glanced down at her tense face and misinterpreted the reason for it. 'Surely the pleasant evening we've spent together proves that you have no reason to fear me, that I can restrain myself from ripping your clothes off, so what's the reason for your frantic rush?'

'You are,' she flung at him furiously, overwhelmed by the stark memory of how he had frequently ignored buttons and fastenings and simply torn her clothing from her body in his desperate fervour to possess her. The air between them crackled with electricity, her heart was pounding, and for the life of her she couldn't drag her gaze from his face.

'I see.' His eyes were hooded and unfathomable, his voice so indifferent that she felt like crawling under a stone, but the arms that tightened around her told a different story, and she gasped when he hauled her close, allowing her to feel the rigid proof of his arousal. 'I think we're both suffering from the same ailment,' he murmured as he lowered his head, his mouth hot and hard on hers, denying her the chance to resist, although, God help her, she tried. 'We always communicated better without words, *cara*,' he told her as she opened her mouth to argue and he captured her denial with his tongue.

Instantly, Eden was transported back to a time when his heated outbursts of temper had ended in passion, anger swiftly replaced by desire, and heat flooded through her body, pooling between her thighs. For the sake of her sanity she should fight him, the voice in her head insisted, but as he lifted her into his arms the room spun, and she curled her arms around his neck. He smelled so good, *tasted* so good, she thought as her face was pressed into his neck and she explored the faint stubble on his chin with her tongue.

'Who needs words when we have this?' Rafe whispered as he sank onto the sofa and drew her down to his lap, his mouth trailing a line of kisses along her neck to the valley between her breasts. 'You are so beautiful, *cara mia*, and I have missed you so much.' His lips found hers once again and coaxed them apart so that his tongue could probe between them in an erotic exploration that made her tremble. She was unaware that he had slid the strap of her dress over her shoulder until she felt the cool air on her breast, but before she could murmur a protest he cupped the soft mound in his hand and she closed her eyes as sensation ripped through her. He drew the zip of her dress down so that the bodice fell to her waist, and she held her breath as he lowered his head and took one hard peak into his mouth. Pleasure engulfed her and she arched her back, linking her hands around his neck to hold him to his task of suckling her.

'Your breasts were always incredibly sensitive,' he said thickly as he transferred his attention to her other nipple, but she was beyond speech, beyond conscious thought, and she groaned when his tongue tormented the throbbing peak, her fingers scrabbling with his shirt buttons in her desperation to feel the warmth of his body against hers.

His bronzed skin was beaded with sweat that dampened

the whorls of dark chest hair, and she ran her hands hungrily over him, feeling the thud of his heart beneath her fingertips. Her dress was split to mid-thigh on the side of her uninjured leg, but when she felt his hand slide beneath her skirt she tensed. Instantly, he sensed her withdrawal and his lips sought hers again, stroking over them, slow and sweet, before deepening the kiss so that she was utterly lost, and she sighed her pleasure when she felt his fingers move beyond the lace band at the top of her stocking to settle on the quivering flesh of her inner thigh.

It had been so long, she thought feverishly, her body on fire as she felt him ease his hand beneath her silk thong. All the time she had been working abroad, ordinary emotions like passion and desire had been buried deep in her subconscious, but as Rafe gently caressed her they flooded back and she clung to him, desperate for him to touch her even more intimately.

'You see, *cara*,' he whispered, 'this is how we communicate best. You want me—your body doesn't lie, see?' He parted her tenderly and slid his finger in deep, watching the way she arched and pushed against him. She was ready for him, hot and moist, and he was overwhelmed with the urge to tear off his clothes and take what she was offering. No woman had ever affected him the way Eden did, and he shifted uncomfortably, trying to ease the ache in his loins. Her perfume, a light, floral fragrance, assailed his senses and he buried his face in her neck, breathing her in. He wanted to push her back against the cushions and drag her long skirt aside to reveal those long, shapely limbs he remembered so well. He wanted to plunge into her and feel her muscles close around his shaft. Just the thought of it made him so hard that he was sure he would explode, but he was aware that he needed to take things slowly.

She was so responsive, such an innately sensual woman, that she must have had other lovers during the past four years. The idea made his body clench; she was his woman, *his*, and he was determined that she would never forget it. He would use all his skill and expertise to bind her to him. He knew how to please her and he felt a surge of primitive satisfaction as he moved his fingers inside her and felt her muscles contract. She was breathing hard, her whole body tense and trembling, and the speed of her climax took him by surprise. Perhaps there hadn't been many other lovers and suddenly he didn't care, from now on there would only be him. Her sobbing gasps of pleasure turned him on and he vowed that her cries would be heard for the rest of the night as he wrung every ounce of pleasure from her body.

Eden came back to earth to find that Rafe had eased her off his lap and she was lying on the sofa with the bodice of her dress down around her waist. For a moment she closed her mind to the voice that warned her she was on a path she was going to regret following. But how could she regret this? This was Rafe, the only man she had ever loved, and making love with him felt so right. Her body had waited patiently for him for four years but it wouldn't wait any longer; she needed him now.

'You don't know how often I've dreamed of you wrapping your long legs around me, *cara*,' he murmured, and his words shattered the spell. His hand slid up her uninjured leg and he hooked his fingers around the top of her stocking, intent on drawing the sheer hose down. She tensed, desire quickly replaced by panic. He was expecting to remove her stockings and reveal the slender, tanned legs he had so admired. She couldn't bear to watch the revulsion that would surely cross his face when he saw her scars.

'Rafe, no, I can't.' She pushed his hand away and sat up, frantically trying to adjust the straps of her dress.

For a second Rafe frowned, but then his expression cleared and he took her hand to draw her to her feet. 'I agree, *cara*. I don't want our first time together after all the years apart to be a hurried fumble on the sofa. I want to make love to you all night in the comfort of a double bed, before we fly to Portugal tomorrow.'

'Portugal!' Eden stared at him as if he'd suddenly grown another head. 'I'm not going to Portugal.'

Rafe was already tugging her towards his room, seemingly oblivious to the dismay in her eyes, and he sighed when she pulled her hand free.

'I know it's sudden but the next two races are back to back—Portugal and then the Italian Grand Prix at Monza. I'm sorry, *cara*, but there'll still be time for us, I promise you.' He tilted her chin and bestowed a brief, hard kiss on her mouth. His lips were warm and enticing and for a moment Eden closed her eyes and gave rein to the fantasy that involved walking into his bedroom and allowing passion to consume her in its fiery blaze.

'Rafe, I'm not going to Portugal or anywhere else, least of all your bedroom.' With a supreme effort she put some space between them and he dropped his hand to his side, his eyes suddenly hooded as the silence between them thrummed with tension.

'What do you mean, *cara*?' he asked, but she wasn't fooled by his deceptively quiet tone and shivered at the hardness in his eyes. 'You know I'm committed to compete for the remainder of this season. How can we maintain any kind of relationship if you refuse to travel with me, or do you expect me to fly back to England whenever I have the chance?'

'I don't expect you to do anything. Why do you expect that you can just walk back into my life and demand that I rearrange it around you?'

'Obviously I mistook your eager response as an indication that you wanted to give our relationship another chance,' Rafe said coldly. 'I didn't realise that you were looking for a one-night stand.'

'I wasn't looking for anything—you started it…' She broke off, miserably aware that even if she hadn't made the first move she'd practically screamed her eagerness from the rooftops.

'At least be honest, Eden,' he taunted. 'Sexual frustration is nothing to be ashamed of. If you just want to scratch an itch, that's fine with me.'

'So you want to give our relationship another chance, do you, Rafe?' Eden hissed. 'But how amazing. Nothing's changed. You still expect me to make all the compromises, to follow you around the world, flaunted in the papers as your blonde tart and held at the mercy of your father's contempt.'

'My father is a good man, a great man, and I won't have you sully his reputation with your spite,' Rafe threw at her, his black eyes burning with fury. 'We had something good, something more than just great sex,' he said more quietly, his nostrils flaring with the effort of controlling his temper. 'We could have it again, *cara*, but not while you maintain this hate campaign against the man I respect more than any other. I wouldn't be where I am today without him,' he told her, his voice ringing with emotion. 'I'm trying very hard to accept that I misjudged you four years ago, and that it was Gianni who lied to me, not you. But it's difficult,' he admitted rawly. 'I loved him, yet in the end I couldn't save him or make him happy enough to want to continue his life. Isn't it enough that you've made me doubt my own brother? Don't start on my father, too.'

'So what are you suggesting?' Eden queried tightly. 'That we pick up where we left off, our affair played out in every tabloid that sees us as easy pickings? What did we really have, anyways, other than an energetic love life?'

'We had more than that,' he insisted, and she shook her head sadly as memories crowded back.

'Did we? Most of the time I was bored and lonely. The focal point of my day was when you came back from the track, and I was so unsure of myself, of my place in your life, that I was desperate for your attention. I turned into someone I didn't like very much,' she whispered. 'I was clingy and pathetic, always looking over my shoulder to see who you might be planning to replace me with. I don't want to become that person again, Rafe, and despite what you think I don't want you.'

It would be eminently satisfying to make her eat those words, Rafe thought darkly, and he could, they both knew. Even now she couldn't disguise her quiver of awareness when he moved closer. It would be so easy to sweep her into his arms and carry her to his bed. Her physical resistance would be minimal, but mentally it would be a different matter, and when he made love to her he intended that there would be no barriers between them.

'In that case I'd better help you to your room,' he said coldly, fighting the urge to plunder that wide, sexy mouth with his, to force his tongue between her soft lips and to hell with the consequences.

'I can manage, thanks.'

'*Dio!* Do you have to argue about everything?' His cool was being sorely tested! He wanted to *shake* her until every stubborn, obstinate bone in her body rattled, and with a muttered oath he pulled her into his arms and strode into her bedroom. 'Dr Hillier said you have prescription painkillers, I suggest you take them,' he said shortly, concern replacing his frustration as he noted the shadows in her eyes and the purple smudges beneath them. She looked all in, infinitely fragile, and he wanted to wrap her in cotton wool, although he was sure he'd receive a physical assault if he tried.

'I don't need any pills. I'm just tired, that's all, and stressed,' she added pointedly.

'Make that an order rather than a suggestion. Where are they—in your handbag or the bathroom?'

He was the bitter end, Eden thought furiously, refusing to admit that she felt nauseous and faint with pain. How dare he accuse her of trying to blacken his father's name, when Fabrizzio had done his best to ruin her reputation and had actually labelled her a whore? The Santini blood ran thick, she conceded bleakly, and she was an outsider who could never come between father and son, brother and brother—she didn't even want to try.

'You have two minutes to get into bed while I get you a

glass of water,' he warned from the doorway. 'Any longer and I'll strip you myself, and who knows where that might lead, *cara mia*?'

She had already slipped off her shoes, and the sound of his mocking laughter goaded her into picking one up and hurling it across the room, her disappointment acute when it missed his head.

'When did you gain that temper?' he queried, amusement gleaming in his eyes, and she glared at him.

'The year I spent with you would have incited a saint to commit murder. You were an inspired tutor, Rafe.'

'I'm glad you think so, *cara*, although I think we may be referring to different subjects!'

She should have known that in a verbal sparring match she was no contest for his acerbic wit, she conceded as she struggled out of her dress and into her nightshirt, anxious to ensure she was safely under the covers before he returned.

'What happens now?' she asked huskily when she had swallowed the two tablets under his watchful gaze.

'I go to my bedroom and you go to sleep, with my assurance that I won't disturb your dreams.'

If only! He'd done so for the last four years, why should tonight be any different?

'I mean between us,' she qualified awkwardly. 'I meant what I said, Rafe, there's no future for us.' She wished she could read the expression in those unfathomable black depths, wished she knew what he was really thinking. 'I'll move out of the Dower House as soon as possible.'

His careless shrug screamed his indifference, and she felt a sharp pain in her chest. This really was the end. He'd run out of patience with her—hardly surprising when she'd led him on and then rejected him tonight—and the reality of seeing him walk out of her life for the second time caused tears to well in her eyes.

'There's no rush; I'll be away for the rest of the summer at least and there's a year's lease to run on the house. My driver will take you back to Wellworth when you're ready in the morning, but I have an early flight, so I'll try not to disturb you.'

She must need her head tested, Eden thought dismally as she stared at the proud tilt of his head. Rafe Santini, the man who was idolised by women the world over, had asked her to be his mistress and she had turned him down! Most women would jump at the chance to travel to exotic locations with a sexy, handsome millionaire lover, but she had tried it once and concluded that she wasn't like most women. She wasn't interested in the high-profile lifestyle and certainly wasn't interested in the money. She didn't want to spend her life shopping for clothes that she hoped would retain her lover's interest and prevent his eyes from straying to the countless wannabes who hung around the track. She just wanted the man, she conceded sadly. She wanted Rafe to love her as she loved him, but his arrogant assumption that he could click his fingers and she would jump to his bidding was proof that nothing had changed. He hadn't loved her four years ago. She doubted he had ever loved any woman. His first love was for racing, for speed and excitement, and the thrill of danger was his overriding mistress.

She needed him to leave her room now, before she did something stupid like throw herself into his arms and promise to become his lover for however long he wanted her. Pride was her only defence against his magnetic pull, and she lifted her chin, determined to hide the fact that she was on shaky ground. 'I guess this is goodbye,' she whispered, and was rewarded with an insolent smile.

'For now, *cara*, but not for long, I think,' he said, his accent very pronounced as he strolled towards the bed. 'How long will it take, I wonder, for you to grow bored with your lonely bed? You'll come back to me, Eden. I know you too well and that passionate nature of yours will make your life hell. I look forward to the day that you come crawling back, *cara mia*. You'll beg me to make you mine again because you belong to me.'

He leaned across the bed and her cry of outraged denial was muffled beneath the force of his lips as he initiated a kiss that was a flagrant assault of her senses. She *hated* him, hated every arrogant, cocksure bone in his body, but by the time she had recovered sufficiently to tell him, he had gone.

CHAPTER SEVEN

WALKING through the front door of the Dower House was like returning to an old friend, Eden thought as she stared up at the mellow, ivy-covered walls that she had so quickly grown to love. Her heart seemed destined to remain in pieces—she couldn't stay in the house and she couldn't have Rafe, although she would happily live in a shoebox if he showed any signs that he wanted more from a relationship with her than just sex.

She handed Nev her formal notice to leave the house, with the request that he keep her posted on any suitable properties she could rent, and after one look at her drawn features he wisely hid his curiosity. Fortunately, summer was a busy time in Wellworth and she spent the remainder of the week covering the vicarage fête, a veterans' cricket match and a scoop about bad drains at the local hospital. After three years reporting on drought and disaster in Africa, it was hard to drum up much enthusiasm for parochial life. Her career was important, she reminded herself. She'd given it up once, caught up in the heady excitement of her romance with Rafe, and she was determined not to sacrifice it again.

If she was honest, she couldn't drum up much enthusiasm for anything, and certainly not food. Her clothes were hanging off her and several friends had asked if she was ill. Only lovesick, she thought grimly—for the second time in four years. But the truth was she hadn't gotten over Rafe the first time and meeting him again had lacerated her already-wounded heart.

She was determined to avoid the television coverage of the Portuguese Grand Prix, and spent the whole of Sunday with Cliff and Jenny and their new baby. She was incredibly lucky, she told herself. She had wonderful friends and lived in one of the most beautiful villages in England. Life was good, and much simpler without Rafe in it, yet later that night she found herself flicking television channels from an amusing comedy to a programme showing highlights of the day's sporting events.

Rafe was in pole position for the start of the race and she experienced the familiar sick feeling in the pit of her stomach as she watched him streak out ahead of all the other cars. Unable to sit still, she wandered edgily between the living room and kitchen, the sudden shout of the commentator causing her to spill an entire carton of orange juice as she shot back to the screen.

'…Santini's off. Rafe Santini, five times World Champion, has crashed at the Portuguese Grand Prix, and I have to say that, from the pictures I'm getting from the scene, it would be a miracle if he emerges from the wreck of his car.'

'No, please, no,' Eden whispered. Where was Rafe? She couldn't see past the throng of track officials but, as the commentator said, it seemed impossible that he could have survived the crash that had left his car a twisted pile of metal.

The programme was showing the highlights, she suddenly remembered. The race had taken place hours before. Rafe could have been dead for hours and she hadn't even known!

'Rafe, get out of the car,' she begged, her heart pounding, and suddenly, incredibly, the crowd of track officials parted and the camera focused on him easing himself out of the protective pod that contained the driver's seat. As he was helped away from the track, the camera closed in on him and Eden sank to her knees in front of the screen. His face was hidden beneath his helmet, so all she could see were his eyes, but as she reached out and touched his image he seemed to stare straight at her and she felt as though she were drowning in those dark, unfathomable depths.

In an instant his image was gone. The programme covered the remainder of the race and then switched to a rugby match, but Eden saw nothing, heard nothing. Shock, fear and ultimately relief had left her so drained that she simply sat in front of the television, her hand resting on the screen as if she could somehow reach through it and touch him. Slowly, she uncurled her legs, wincing as cramps gripped her muscles, and she staggered upstairs, not to her bedroom but to the master suite Rafe had slept in for one night. The misery that she'd held in check all week broke over her in a wave and she cried until her chest hurt and her eyes were red-rimmed. So this was love, she thought bitterly. This agonising fear for his safety and a clawing desperation to jump on the next flight and follow him to whichever corner of the world he was in.

She couldn't live without him, she acknowledged wearily, but neither could she live with him. How could she even contemplate returning to life as his mistress, moving constantly from hotel to hotel and waiting, always waiting for him to finish a race, a Press interview or a function in his honour before she was able to grab his attention for a few brief hours? It seemed that shè was forever destined to love a man who was out of her reach, because Rafe didn't love her; she doubted that he ever had. The question that kept her awake for the rest of he night was, could she settle for anything less?

The Italian Grand Prix was staged at Monza and the roads leading to the racetrack were heavily congested, despite the fact that the race wasn't due to start for several hours. Rafe's personal assistant, Petra—a woman who would one day surely be canonised in recognition of her patience—had listened to Eden's request for a ticket to the race without asking any difficult questions. Discretion was Petra's byword and no doubt a necessary part of her job as she tried to unravel Rafe's love life, Eden thought bleakly. But Petra had been one of her few allies during her time with the Santini team, and the following day a VIP ticket and flight details had arrived at the Dower House.

The rest was up to her, Eden acknowledged, and fear lurched sickly in the pit of her stomach. She must be mad, walking of her own accord into the lion's den, and quite possibly Rafe would reject her, but since she'd witnessed his accident she'd been forced to accept that her life without him was no life at all.

Her ticket included a champagne reception and she was whisked off to the VIP box by an official, her heart sinking at the bevy of beautiful women around her. Monza was a big event in Italy's social calendar and the room was full of high-ranking members of Italian society, plus the usual array of models and glamour girls that followed the Formula 1 scene. She couldn't compete, Eden thought bleakly, ready to turn tail and run. Some of the women were truly stunning, tall, tanned, with impossibly long legs and incredibly short skirts. Rafe liked women in skirts—he thought trousers were unfeminine—but Eden had had no option but to wear a trouser suit to hide her scars.

The ice-blue suit had been ruinously expensive but worth every penny for its superb cut, the trousers skimming her curves while the jacket emphasised her slender waist. She looked cool and elegant yet innately sensual with her lacy camisole just visible beneath the jacket, and her hair caught up in a loose chignon.

Compared to the skimpily dressed women in the VIP box, she looked like one of the vestal virgins, Eden decided, but pride forced her to hold her head high and she smiled as she recognised one of the mechanics from the Santini team.

Alonso spoke little English and she wasn't even sure he would remember her after all this time, but as she approached him he grinned and ran his eyes over her, his admiration clearly evident.

'I've come to see Rafe,' she began hesitantly, and he shrugged but picked up on the one word he understood.

'Rafe? You come. He's on the grid.'

Before the start of a race the grid was packed with track officials and celebrities mingling with the drivers. Monza was a big race for Rafe, before his home crowd. He was a legendary figure in Italy and thousands of fans flocked to see him win. Failing them wasn't an option and the sense of excited anticipation in the air emphasised to Eden the intense pressure he was under.

He was leaning against his car, dressed in a white race suit decorated with the logos of his many sponsors, a white cap jammed on his head. He looked bronzed and fit, his black hair just visible from beneath the cap, his eyes gleaming like polished jet as he laughed with the photographers. Around him was a group of stunning, bikini-clad girls, the sashes across their voluptuous bodies displaying the logo of the company they were advertising.

'OK, Rafe, if you could put your arm round Cindy's waist, and Cindy, snuggle up to him, sweetheart, that's it, put your hand on his chest. Great shot, and again.'

At the edge of the group was the one man Eden had hoped not to see, and her heart sank as she stared at Fabrizzio Santini. A Sicilian by birth, Fabrizzio was several inches shorter than his son, but with the same broad shoulders and strong jaw. The son of a peasant farmer made good. His rise to the top, and as the force behind the Santini car company, were well-documented, as was the fact that his marriage to a wealthy heiress had much to do with his success. Even now, with a billion-pound fortune to his name, he possessed a ruthless streak that business rivals feared. He took what he wanted from life, discarding anything he deemed not good enough, and Eden had been top of his junk pile.

'Hey, boss!' Alonso called cheerfully, and Rafe turned his head, his whole body stiffening as he stared at Eden. 'Signorina Eden's back.'

'Is that so?' Rafe crossed his arms over his chest and let his gaze trawl over Eden in a slow appraisal as if she were a particularly curious specimen in a jar. Around him the girls stopped chattering and the photographers fiddled with their cameras, the nuance in Rafe's voice warning them to be ready for what might be an interesting shot. 'This is a surprise,' he drawled. 'What do you want, Eden?'

Beneath his indolent stance he was tense, aggression emanating from every pore, his eyes cold and hard as he waited for her to speak.

'You,' Eden replied simply. She didn't know what else to say other than the truth.

She had the interest of everyone in the crowd now and the models giggled and moved closer to Rafe. The sun beat down mercilessly, forming a shimmering heat haze on the tarmac, and all around race marshals scurried like busy ants. There was no way she could come out of this with any vestige of pride intact, Eden acknowledged as she stared at Rafe and remembered his taunts that she would one day crawl back to him. There was no chink of softness in his expression; he was hard and unrelenting, bristling with injured male pride at the way she had rejected him, and she sighed. He wasn't going to make this easy but her pride had already suffered its last death throes, and abject humiliation before a crowd of gorgeous blondes wasn't going to make much difference now.

'You said you would enjoy seeing me beg for a chance to come back to you,' she reminded him steadily, her eyes focused only on him. 'Well, here I am, begging.'

The giggling grew bolder. A couple of photographers snapped shots of Eden, but she didn't spare them a glance and it was Rafe who moved impatiently, shrugging out of Cindy's hold while a nerve jumped in his cheek.

'No more photos,' he demanded, 'we've finished now.' He strode off, only pausing for a second to glare at Eden. 'Are you coming, or not?' he snapped, and hastily she stumbled after him, unable to decipher his reaction and unaware that Fabrizzio Santini's speculative gaze followed them both.

His trailer was far from luxurious. He might be a multi-millionaire, but there were no airs and graces to him, and he preferred to hang out with the other members of the team. Once inside he headed for the fridge, extracted a bottle of water and flipped the lid before taking a swig.

'Just what the hell are you playing at, Eden?' he growled as he leaned against a cupboard and surveyed her grimly. 'Two weeks ago you were adamant you wanted nothing more to do with me. Why the sudden change of heart?'

'I miss you,' she replied honestly. During the long, sleepless night after his crash, she'd finally concluded that life was too short and precarious. It was only the most incredible luck that had seen her escape with her life after the land-mine explosion, the same luck that meant he'd climbed out of the car unhurt in Portugal. What if one day their luck ran out? she wondered. Wasn't it time to follow her heart rather than her head?

Rafe gave a disbelieving snort and paced the trailer restlessly, pulling his cap from his head and raking his hand through his hair. 'Is that the truth?' he demanded, but beneath the arrogance she caught the faint note of uncertainty in his husky voice, and her heart turned over. He didn't do uncertain, he was the most self-assured man on the planet, yet, incredible though it seemed, her answer mattered to him. Despite the attentions of every gorgeous woman on the circuit, Rafe still wanted *her*.

'I'm not playing at anything,' she promised as she walked towards him. 'All I want is this.' Taking a deep breath, she reached up on tiptoe and drew his head down, her lips seeking his with an air of self-possession that hid her quaking nerves.

He smelled so good—warm and male—the exotic musk of his aftershave stirring her senses. For what seemed an eternity he made no response, his hands clenched by his sides, his mouth set in an inflexible line, and with a growing sense of desperation Eden deepened the kiss, her tongue exploring the contours of his lips before tentatively dipping between them. She'd misread the signs, came the agonising realisation. He didn't want her, and in a few seconds he would thrust her from him, crucify her with his contempt. But just as she was ready to admit defeat, he groaned low in his throat and his arms clamped round her, pulling her hard against him.

As his lips parted Eden felt almost faint with relief, and she sagged against him, allowing him to take control, and he kissed her with a hungry passion that demanded her response.

This was where she was meant to be, she thought with an almost fatalistic acceptance. She was Rafe's woman, and despite the years apart he was the only man she would ever want.

'This time there will be no going back, no changing your mind at the last minute,' Rafe warned when at last he lifted his head and she dragged oxygen into her lungs. 'I'm so desperate for you I could take you right now, in a trailer in the middle of the bloody Grand Prix, and to hell with whoever walks in on us.' He inhaled sharply, his nostrils flaring with the effort of enforcing control over his desire, and Eden reached up to stroke his jaw. 'There's no time, as usual,' he muttered. 'There was never any time for us.'

'We'll make time,' she promised. 'After the race, I'll be here, waiting for you.'

He muttered something in Italian before his mouth captured hers once more and he ran his hands over her body in a fevered exploration, unfastening her jacket to slip inside, and he growled his pleasure when he discovered the delicate camisole and the indubitable proof that she wasn't wearing a bra. '*Cara mia*, I want you so badly I will explode with it,' he muttered rawly, and Eden couldn't disguise her shiver of excitement when he stroked her nipples through the sheer silk of her camisole. She wanted more, wanted him to strip her and take her *now*, but a huge crowd of fans had gathered to see their nation's hero, and her time would come later.

'I'll be here,' she vowed once more, and the rap on the door of the trailer warned her that she would have to contain her impatience, although Rafe's muttered curse told her he was also struggling.

'Why have you really come?' he asked again as he jammed his cap on his head and pulled the peak low, hiding his eyes.

'I watched the Portuguese Grand Prix. You were the high-light of the day.' She closed her eyes briefly, reliving those terrifying moments before she had seen him climb out of the car.

'I wasn't hurt, *cara*, a few bruises, that's all.'

'I know—I spoke to Petra afterwards. But what if you hadn't survived, Rafe? All I would have is my pride. You said you wanted to give our relationship another chance, a fresh start.' She hesitated for a moment and then whispered, 'I want that, too. I'm tired of thinking about the past or worrying about the future, and I don't know how long it'll last between us, but quite frankly I don't care any more. I want you now, today,' she told him firmly, and his mouth curved into the slow, sexy smile she adored.

'I'm a little busy right now, *cara mia*. Can you wait until tonight?'

The Villa Mimosa was situated a half-hour drive away from Milan, in a small village on the shores of Lake Como. The master suite, at the front of the villa, afforded stunning views across the sparkling blue water of the lake, while the back looked over a fabulous private garden and pool. It was an oasis of tranquillity, yet surprisingly close to cosmopolitan Milan, which boasted designer shops and magnificent architecture.

Returning to the villa was like stepping back in time and as Eden glanced around the master suite she was assailed by memories. In this room, she had known heaven and hell! During the year she had spent with Rafe the villa had been home, although they had spent little time in it, but for a few precious weeks after the end of the racing season when she had revelled in the intimacy of sharing his bedroom. Rafe had no doubt employed top interior designers to decorate the villa, but the decor of his suite was unchanged, even to the collection of glass frogs on the dressing table, and Eden felt a curious pain in her chest as she picked one up. They were cheap and gaudy, made from green glass, but she had fallen in love with them in a marketplace in Spain and had been delighted when Rafe had bought them for her. Why had he kept them? she wondered. They looked painfully out of place in the elegant room, but for some reason he had them on prominent display, and she wondered if he ever thought of her when he looked at them.

She set the frog back in its place and studied her reflection in the dressing-table mirror. She had bought the sexy black negligee for one purpose only—seduction—and she had to admit that she looked the part of a sensual siren, but inside she was so nervous she felt sick. It had been midnight by the time they were able to leave the after-race party, and, as the winner of the Monza Grand Prix, Rafe had been in huge demand. Eden had attempted to keep out of the limelight, but he would have none of it and kept her clamped to his side all evening, arousing the curiosity of the Press photographers. Now, finally, they had some privacy, but as the car had swung onto the driveway of the villa she had been beset with nerves, and gladly accepted Rafe's suggestion of a shower.

'Did you find everything you required in the bathroom?'

The sound of his voice caused her to whirl away from the mirror, eyes wide, the pulse at the base of her throat setting up a frantic tattoo as she stared at him. 'Yes, thank you.' She had been stunned to discover her favourite range of toiletries set out in the bathroom, but had told herself it must be coincidence; Rafe was hardly likely to have remembered the fragrance she had used five years ago.

He strolled across the room to extract a bottle of champagne from the ice bucket, and her eyes were drawn to the width of his shoulders, his white silk shirt open at the throat to reveal an expanse of olive skin. If anything, he was even more devastatingly attractive than five years ago. His body was leaner, harder, and the bold expression in his eyes caused a familiar weakness to flood through her. His eyes were telling her that he would make love to her tonight, that there would be no reprieve, and the thought filled her with nervous anticipation, an excitement she could no longer deny.

Rafe's eyes narrowed as he released the champagne cork, noting the way Eden jumped liked a startled doe at the sound. She was not as self-assured as she would have him believe, but he liked that, liked the fact that she was nervous about their first time together after all the years apart. It mirrored his own tension. *Dio!* She was beautiful, he thought as he handed her a glass. He'd fantasised about her body all day, imagined the fullness of her breasts and her long, slender legs which were hidden beneath her trousers. The negligee left little to the imagination and his fingers itched to untie the ribbons that laced the bodice so that her breasts spilled from the black silk. The gown was floor-length, hiding her legs, but not for long, he acknowledged, his heart rate quickening as he mentally stripped her.

He intended to take it slow, to savour every delicious moment, but already he was so aroused that his trousers felt uncomfortably tight and he was filled with a primitive urge to rip the enticing scrap of black silk from her body and take her hard and fast, make her his in a way she would never forget.

'I think tonight calls for a toast,' he murmured, his eyes never leaving her face as he raised his glass. 'To us, Eden— for as long as it lasts.'

His words caused a sliver of ice to run down Eden's spine, but she took a sip of champagne before obediently agreeing.

'For as long as it lasts,' she said coolly, and anything else she might have said was lost beneath the pressure of his mouth. He tasted of champagne, and her already heightened senses went into overdrive as he forced his tongue between her lips in a fierce exploration that forewarned her of his hunger and his overriding need to possess her. She was on fire for him instantly. There was no slow build-up of passion, just a whoosh, like setting a flame to tinder, and she ran her hands over him, her fingers fumbling with his shirt buttons in her feverish desperation to touch his skin. Beneath her fingertips she could feel his heart pounding in his chest. He wasn't as in control as he made out, not quite the all-conquering master he portrayed, but a man enslaved by the burning passion that consumed them both.

'You fill my senses until I can think of nothing but you,' he muttered against her throat when at last he lifted his head and trailed his mouth down to the valley between her breasts. His fingers tugged impatiently at the ribbon that secured the bodice of her negligee, his hands cupping her breasts, moulding them and lifting them so that he could take first one throbbing peak, and then the other, into his mouth. 'I want you now, *cara*, I can't wait.'

The room spun as he lifted her and laid her on the bed and she watched through half-closed eyes as he shrugged out of his shirt before coming down on top of her. She wanted him, too, wanted him with an urgency that shook her, made her forget, but as she felt him tug the negligee over her hips her memory returned with a vengeance.

'I want to keep it on,' she whispered, and heard his low growl of laughter.

'Not a hope. I have spent the last four years fantasising about your body, the whiteness of your skin spread on black silk sheets, ready for me. I want to see all of you, *cara*, every beautiful inch of those long, sexy legs I remember so well.' With a final tug he discarded the negligee and let his gaze roam her body. *'Madre de Dio!'*

Eden squeezed her eyes closed. Hearing the shock in his voice was bad enough without witnessing the revulsion on his face. 'I warned you my leg wasn't a pretty sight,' she said thickly, striving for a light tone and failing miserably.

Still nothing. Rafe's silence was worse than any kind of verbal rejection, and in an agony of despair she opened her eyes to face the look of horror in his. 'You don't have to… I mean, I'll understand if the urge has gone,' she quipped huskily, and his eyes darkened.

'Why do you think I no longer desire you?' he asked, and she twisted restlessly, wanting to drag her nightgown back over her body to hide her scars. 'Do you really think these,' he traced his finger over the scars that criss-crossed her leg, 'would make any difference to my hunger for you?'

'They're horrible,' Eden whispered, blinking back her tears. It was pathetic to cry, especially when she had witnessed the bravery of people with far worse injuries, but she felt so vulnerable. Rafe could take his pick from the most beautiful women in the world, why on earth would he pick her, now? 'The surgeon said they'll fade a little in time, but my leg's a mess and you always were a leg man,' she finished, unable to disguise the wobble in her voice.

'I was always *your* man,' Rafe told her, so forcefully that she stared at him. 'Is this the reason you rejected me in London?' he asked as realisation dawned, and Eden nodded.

'I thought you would be disgusted and I couldn't bear the fact that you would find me ugly.' She sniffed inelegantly and scrubbed her eyes with the back of her hand. As a passion killer it worked wonders, she thought bleakly. She felt cold and devoid of anything but a need to hide herself away to metaphorically lick her wounds, and despite Rafe's protestations he didn't look like a man overwhelmed by passion, either. 'I'll sleep in the guest suite,' she told him, but as she went to sit up he pushed her back against the pillows.

'Neither of us will be sleeping anywhere, not if I can help it,' he informed her coolly, and she watched with wide eyes as he stood up and unzipped his trousers. He took his time. If it hadn't been such an incredible idea she would have said he was doing it deliberately, stripping in front of her with slow, steady intent, and her mouth ran dry when he slid his boxers over his hips and stood naked and magnificently aroused.

'Rafe, you don't have to…' Eden began and he gave a harsh laugh.

'I think it's rather obvious that I do, *cara.*' He knelt at the end of the bed, lowered his head and feathered a line of kisses along the deep scar that ran the length of her shin.

'Don't,' she pleaded, his touch making her flinch, and he stared into her eyes.

'Does it hurt when I touch them?'

'No,' she admitted, 'but they're hardly attractive.'

'They're part of you,' he said simply, 'and I want you,

all of you. If I looked shocked when I first saw your leg, it was not through disgust, it was…' He broke off, searching for the words. '…Compassion, pain, here inside.' He held his hand against his heart. 'I can't bear to think of you lying somewhere, bloodied and hurt. I wasn't there, I couldn't help you.'

He bent his head once more and this time she forced herself to relax as his lips anointed each scar in gentle benediction. By the time he reached the sensitive flesh of her inner thigh she was breathing hard, desire flooding through her so that she moved her hips restlessly and held her breath when he hooked his fingers around the waistband of her briefs.

'You will always be the most beautiful woman in the world to me, *cara*,' he told her, and even if she had not trusted the words, the burning intensity in his dark eyes revealed the depths of his passion. A mixture of relief and joy filled her, banishing the last of her inhibitions, and she lifted her hips, enabling him to draw her knickers down over her hips.

Her skin was creamy and satin-smooth, an erotic contrast to the black silk sheets, and Rafe surveyed her in silence for a moment, a tide of colour running along his cheekbones. 'Four years is a long time, *cara mia*. Have there been many others?' he queried, his voice such a deep, husky growl she could barely make out the words.

She wanted to say something glib, taunt him that her tally of lovers was hardly likely to match his, but there was a curious vulnerability about the way he refused to meet her gaze and she ran her fingers over his jaw. 'Does it matter?' she whispered, and he shook his head.

'No, you're in my bed now and that's all that matters.' He allowed her to guide his face down to hers, and she smiled against his lips.

'You're the only one, Rafe, the only man I've ever wanted.'

'The only man you'll ever know,' he corrected. 'Promise me you'll stay with me, Eden, for as long as I want you.'

Her reply was lost beneath the force of his lips. Her admission that he was her only lover had opened the floodgates and he claimed her mouth in a devastating assault while his hands roamed her body, down over her stomach to slip between her thighs. She was ready for him, slick and wet, and he pushed her legs apart, sliding his hands beneath her bottom to lift her. He entered her slowly, his body rigid with the effort, but by her own admission it had been a long time and he wanted to give her time to accommodate him. His intentions were good, but she was so tight, felt so good, that he was afraid he would explode, and he stilled and rested his forehead against hers, his brow beaded with sweat.

'I don't want to hurt you, *cara*,' he muttered and inhaled sharply as she wriggled experimentally beneath him.

'The only way you could hurt me is if you stop,' she assured him, and he snatched the remnants of his self-control and began to thrust, deep and slow, waiting for her to match his rhythm before he increased the pace.

Eden clung to his shoulders as he drove into her. It was so good—she had forgotten how good—and she twisted her head from side to side, her body arching as he took her higher and higher until her muscles clenched in a spasm of pleasure that ripped through her. 'Rafe,' she cried brokenly as wave after wave kept coming, each powerful thrust causing her to contract around him, and he groaned, his face a taut mask in the seconds before he shuddered with the force of his release.

'You made a promise to stay for as long as I want you.'

Eden tensed. She didn't know what she had expected his first words to be after they had shared such mind-blowing intimacy and she opened her eyes to stare at him uncertainly. Had it all been a power game after all, and, now that he had won, was he going to tell her that she had served her purpose and he no longer wanted her? 'Yes, I did,' she agreed huskily, and watched as his mouth curved into a sensual smile.

'I'll want you for a long, long time,' he warned her. 'Maybe forever.'

'Then that's how long I'll stay,' she said simply, and his smile faded, his eyes darkening as he captured her lips in a kiss that held tenderness as well as passion.

CHAPTER EIGHT

THE Villa Mimosa boasted a fabulous pool, and for the last few days Eden had found plenty of time to admire it. It was a beautiful Italian summer's day. Rafe's housekeeper, Sophia, was on hand to provide tempting delicacies and her paperback was reasonably entertaining. She had everything she could possibly want, she reminded herself, ignoring the voice in her head that pointed out she didn't have Rafe.

He was there at night, of course. She couldn't complain about his lack of attention in the bedroom, or his passion. He made love to her with single-minded dedication, as if he was determined to make up for the years they'd spent apart. In bed, nothing seemed as important as the way he made her feel, the touch of his hands and mouth on her skin, the way he took her to the very edge of ecstasy, prolonged her agony and then tipped her over. When he made love to her she became a mindless, wanton creature intent only on the giving and receiving of pleasure until she fell into a dreamless sleep in his arms.

Sometimes he woke her in the hour before dawn by the simple method of trailing his lips over her already-sensitised skin. Then she would smile sleepily, her body instantly ready to welcome his as he entered her with slow, deep thrusts that quickly fanned the flames of her desire, but when she stirred later the bed was always empty.

He had commitments; she knew that. The time between races was as crucial as the race itself as he worked closely with the designers and engineers to perfect the car's performance. Now he had the added pressure of heading the Santini business interests. He'd explained that his father had suffered a mild stroke, possibly brought on by the devastation of Gianni's suicide, and Fabrizzio was determined to hand over the reins of power to his remaining son and heir.

She understood all of that, so why did the demon in her head whisper that nothing had changed, that their relationship was based on sex, and nothing else? She was acting like a spoilt child, she told herself. Rafe had always lived his life at a furious pace, both on and off the track; she couldn't realistically have expected things to be any different. She hadn't been happy four years ago, but then she had lacked the confidence to tell him. If their relationship was to stand a chance, she would have to speak out and fight for the kind of life she wanted before her self-respect was eroded as it had been once before.

He arrived back at the villa in time for lunch, and as he strolled across the terrace her heart flipped. He looked utterly gorgeous in chinos and a cream shirt that was open at the throat to reveal an expanse of dark chest hair. With his designer shades and the chunky gold Rolex on his wrist he was every inch the millionaire playboy, not a man who would be content to settle for a life of domestic harmony, she conceded sadly.

'*Buon giorno, cara,*' he greeted, leaning down to capture her mouth in a fierce, hungry kiss that drove everything but him from her mind. 'What have you been doing this morning?'

'Swimming, reading…' She kept her tone deliberately light. 'The exercise and sunshine are good for my leg. The scars are definitely fading a bit.'

He settled on the edge of her sun lounger and ran his hand gently over her injured leg. 'Good, I'm glad for you, but I told you, if the scars upset you I'll arrange an appointment with the best plastic surgeon I can find.'

'Do you want me to have surgery?' she asked curiously. He told her endlessly that she was beautiful with or without her scars, but surely, if he was honest, he would prefer her to have the perfect, smooth limbs she'd once had.

He removed his sunglasses and trapped her gaze, a wealth of gentle emotion in his dark eyes. 'If I'm honest…no. Your scars are part of you, an important reminder of the brave and fearless woman you are. You are perfect to me, *cara*,' he murmured deeply, and tears burned behind her eyelids as he bent his head and trailed a line of kisses along each of the welts that criss-crossed her leg.

His lips moved on upwards over her thighs and she held her breath as he dipped his tongue into the sensitive hollow of her navel. The tenure of his caresses changed and she stirred restlessly on the lounger as he unhooked the clasp of her halter-neck bikini and drew the triangles of material down so that her breasts were exposed to his gaze.

'Sophia said she would bring lunch out onto the terrace,' Eden murmured distractedly, finding it hard to think when he cupped each breast in his hands, his olive-skinned fingers splayed in stark relief against the whiteness of her flesh.

'I told her to wait a while,' he said, his voice laced with amusement and a fierce sexual excitement she had only belatedly recognised.

'But I'm hungry,' she reproached, not bothering to disguise the wicked gleam in her eyes, 'aren't you?'

'Starving, *cara*,' he groaned as he pushed her breasts together, his tongue drawing wet circles around each aureole before he took one hard nub into his mouth. 'Feed me!'

She was on fire for him, desperate for him to discard her bikini pants in the same way that he had done the top, but instead he sat up and ran his fingers down her body, stroking insistently against the clinging Lycra until molten heat flooded between her thighs.

'Rafe! Please…now.' She couldn't wait much longer. He hadn't even touched her intimately, yet she could feel the first delicious spasm of pleasure rip through her and the desire to feel him inside her had spiralled into a desperate, clawing need. Still he sat looking down at her, his eyes hooded as he watched the expression on her face, saw her desperation.

'Lift your hips,' he commanded, his voice as thick as treacle slowly trickling over her, and when she obeyed he pulled her briefs off with quiet intent and ran his hands over her thighs, parting them so that her ankles hung over either side of the lounger. He stood then and stripped, not hurrying, his eyes locked with hers, and she thought she would die with anticipation when he finally lowered himself onto her and entered her with a hard, deliberate thrust. He moved deep within her and then withdrew almost completely so that she gasped his name and dug her nails into his shoulders, urging him to fill her again and matching his steady rhythm. She was so turned on that her control stood no chance and she tipped her head back to stare up at the cloudless sky as sensation built, wave upon wave, her muscles contracting around him, her climax so intense that she sobbed his name and clung on for dear life. He paused momentarily, poised above her, his brow beaded with sweat as he fought for control, and when her first spasms eased he moved again, pumping into her, harder, faster, until he could no longer hold back and felt the glory of release as he spilled inside her.

The sound of his mobile phone shattered the exquisite peace and Eden held her breath as, for a few seconds, Rafe ignored it. He stared into her eyes, his frustration evident, and then muttered an oath and snatched it up.

'Papa.' Instantly he reverted to his native, voluble Italian that Eden couldn't understand, even if she was interested, which she was not. Most of Rafe's phone conversations were with his father and Fabrizzio demanded his son's attention at any hour of the day or, more usually, night. Eden could almost believe he was watching them, somehow spying on them, determined to intrude on the few precious hours they spent alone, and she knew with absolute certainty that Fabrizzio was far from happy about her place in Rafe's life.

She wriggled off the lounger, slid her arms into her robe and headed for the cool of the villa. A shower, something to eat and an afternoon doing…well, she'd think of something, she reassured herself. Rafe would no doubt go to the Santini offices at the behest of his father.

He was waiting in their bedroom when she padded through from the *ensuite*, her hair wrapped in a towel.

'I'm sorry about that. My father—'

'You don't have to explain, I know he's been ill and that you're busy.'

'Not usually this busy,' Rafe murmured, his frown deepening as he swung away from her to stare out of the window. She looked gorgeous, pink and soft, wrapped in a fluffy towel, and he would like nothing better than to unwrap her, inch by delectable inch, and tumble her onto the bed. Their loving would be slow and sensuous this time, but as he felt his body harden in eager anticipation he shut his eyes and willed his hormones into line. Fabrizzio wanted him in the office, ostensibly to go through some paperwork that had suddenly been elevated to urgent, although he couldn't understand the reason why.

For the first time in his life he resented the demands Fabrizzio made. If he was honest, he resented anything and anyone that took him away from Eden, and even the hours at the test track suddenly seemed a chore. At the back of his mind lurked the accusation Eden had made that his father had despised and insulted her. At first he'd angrily discounted her suggestion that Fabrizzio had actively sought to wreck their relationship and had even involved Gianni in his plans. She must have been mistaken, he assured himself. She had been young and shy; quite possibly she'd felt in awe of Fabrizzio's dominant personality and imagined his dislike. His father had always been courteous towards her, hadn't he? It was true he hadn't welcomed her with open arms, but then he'd never hidden his hope that his eldest son would marry an Italian girl. A girl like Valentina de Domenici!

'I have a few days clear before the Indianapolis Grand Prix,' he said as he watched her dress. 'I thought we could explore Venice.'

'Really?' Pleasure glowed in her eyes before her lashes swept down to conceal her emotions. 'Don't you have things to do? Your father…'

'Can manage without me for a few days. Four years ago I made the mistake of not spending enough time with you. I don't want to go down that route again, but I'm afraid I'll be out for the rest of today.'

'Luckily I have a good book,' she said cheerfully, as she anticipated the pleasure of a few whole days and nights of his exclusive company in Venice.

'You could go out,' he muttered, wishing he could stay with her and they could barricade themselves in against the rest of the world. 'You could go shopping. Milan is world-renowned for its exclusive boutiques and most women like to shop,' he finished on a note of frustration that she didn't fit the mould.

'You said you liked me because I'm different,' she reminded him with a smile. 'I'm not interested in your money, Rafe,' she told him softly as she linked her arms around his neck. 'I'm just interested in you.'

Venice had lived up to its reputation as one of the world's most romantic cites, Eden mused as she stretched beneath the tangled sheets and stared up at the ornate carvings that decorated the four-poster bed. She would have been content to remain at the villa, but Rafe was determined to honour a promise he'd made four years before and they'd spent a blissful few days exploring the network of canals that wound through the city.

While the days had been spent absorbing the rich history and culture of Venice, the nights had been no less energetic, and Eden's body ached pleasurably. Rafe's desire for her was like a bottomless well, but she wasn't complaining, and even though he had made love to her several times during the night she smiled at the memory of how he liked to spend his mornings. She rolled over, her smile fading when she discovered the bed empty.

A breeze lifted the voile curtain and she glimpsed him, sitting on one of the ornate chairs on the balcony where they ate breakfast each morning.

'You're up early,' she murmured, coming to stand behind him and sliding her arms over his shoulders.

He made no reply but caught hold of one of her hands and held it to his mouth, his lips warm against the pulse point at her wrist.

'I've been thinking,' he murmured at last, and she felt a *frisson* of apprehension run the length of her spine. Thinking had an ominous ring to it. 'About the past, you and Gianni,' he added quietly.

'I thought we'd agreed to live firmly in the present, but there never was a me and Gianni. I wasn't kissing him by the pool that night and I didn't have an affair with him.'

'I believe you, *cara*,' he said heavily. 'I should have known then that you would never lie. You're the most transparent person I've ever met. You don't keep secrets, not from me. Your mind is as clear as a crystal pool.'

She hoped it wasn't that clear: there was one secret she

could never reveal. Love didn't enter into their relationship and she refused to embarrass both of them with the declaration that he was the love of her life.

'I owe you an apology.' He stood and drew her into his arms, his hands gentle as he stroked her hair. 'I don't know why Gianni wanted to break us up, all I can think is that he wanted you for himself and his feelings were so strong that he was prepared to sacrifice his bond with me.' He paused and she felt his lips on her brow, trailing over her cheek to rest at the corner of her mouth. 'We lost four years. Because of him I threw away something that was very precious to me. You,' he told her when she could only stare at him in stunned silence. 'I trusted his word over yours, but I can't hate him for what he did. *Madre de Dio*, Eden, despite the hurt he caused us both, I still wish he was here and I still miss him.'

'I know,' she cried as she flung her arms round him and held him tight. 'I don't hate Gianni and I certainly don't expect you to. He was your brother. I saw how close the two of you were.'

'But why did he try so hard to wreck the thing that made me so happy—my relationship with you? He knew how I felt about you.'

'I don't know, but he must have had a good reason because he idolised you, Rafe.' Someone must have persuaded Gianni to lie, she thought silently, and she had a pretty good idea of who that someone was, but she could hardly voice her suspicions about Fabrizzio to Rafe again—he was already hurting enough. 'It's over now,' she murmured against his neck, 'and despite everything, we've found our way back to each other. I think we should let Gianni and his secrets rest in peace.'

He kissed her then, an evocative caress that stirred her soul with its tenderness, and she wound her arms round his neck as he lifted her and carried her through to the bedroom.

'I think your suggestion that we concentrate on the present rather than the past is an excellent idea,' he told her as he laid her on the sheets and untied the belt of her robe to part the material with deliberate intent. She said nothing, but her eyes darkened, her lips parting slightly as she watched him shrug out of his own robe and come down on the bed beside her.

'You're the only man I've ever wanted, Rafe,' she whispered, aware that she was in danger of revealing too much, but unable to stop herself. For a few moments she'd witnessed the utter devastation he felt at Gianni's death, a sadness that was now compounded by the realisation that his brother had lied to him, and she wanted to comfort him, show him she cared.

He stilled at her words and then ran his hands lightly over her body, gently nudging her legs apart, and she held her breath as he knelt beside her, feeling the warmth of his breath on the sensitive flesh of her inner thigh.

'Then I'd better make sure the situation stays that way, *cara mia*,' he teased, and proceeded to use his tongue with such devastating effect that she was lost to everything but the mastery of his touch.

Rafe dropped the bombshell as his private jet circled over Milan, preparing to land. He'd spent most of the flight with his mobile phone clamped to his ear and, although she'd been unable to understand much of his conversation, Eden gathered from the terseness of his voice that he wasn't happy. Their few blissful days together were over and reality was pounding on the door.

'I'm hosting a dinner party at the villa tonight, nothing too grand, just a handful of business associates.'

Eden stared at him, unable to hide her dismay. 'How big is a handful?'

He gave a careless shrug. 'Twenty or so guests.'

'Do you think you could have given me a little more notice?' she demanded, the surge of panic that swept through her making her snappy. 'How am I going to organise a dinner party in a couple of hours? You know I can't cook.'

'You don't have to do anything, *cara*. It's Sophia's job to deal with these things, and out of kindness to her I ask that you keep well away from the kitchen.'

'Thanks,' Eden said huffily. She might be a hopeless cook but he didn't have to emphasise the point. She felt hurt that he hadn't found it necessary to consult her. It brought home how unimportant she was in his life. He didn't need her, that much was obvious, especially when he had his unflappable housekeeper to deal with his domestic arrangements. She felt like a spare part, superfluous to requirements except in the bedroom, and he couldn't have shouted any louder that to him she was simply his mistress. 'I still think you might have warned me,' she muttered, and he sighed.

'I didn't know myself. My father only sprang it on me this morning that he'd arranged for the dinner to take place at the villa rather than his own home.'

Fabrizzio, again—Eden sniffed. 'Does he often do things like that, expect you to be constantly at his beck and call?'

Never before, was the truthful answer, and Rafe stared

moodily out of the window as the limousine whisked them back to the villa. 'My father's been ill, the heart scare last year shook him, and he's no longer a young man,' he told her shortly. 'It's understandable that he wants me to increase my involvement in the Santini business. I can't race forever and, now that Gianni's gone, I am the sole heir.'

His phone rang again, demanding his attention for the remainder of the journey, and he gave her a distracted glance when they arrived at the villa.

'You don't have to worry about a thing, *cara*. Everything's taken care of. Why don't you relax by the pool for a couple of hours until the guests arrive?'

'Next you'll be patting my bottom and telling me not to bother my pretty little head,' she snapped furiously. 'I know where I'm not wanted, Rafe. I'll just keep out of the way. Are you sure you can put up with my embarrassing presence at dinner, or would you rather send a bowl of gruel up to my room later?'

'*Dio!* You have developed the tongue of a viper,' he roared, his temper exploding like a volcanic eruption, his accent very pronounced as he rounded on her. 'Four years ago you would never have—'

'Answered back?' she suggested sweetly, and received a furious glare.

'I'm sorry I didn't let you know earlier about the dinner party,' he stated more quietly as he took a deep breath. 'But it's only for a few hours, and you're behaving like a spoilt child.'

'I know,' she yelled. She really didn't need him to point it out so she swung her back on him and marched out to the pool. As she passed him he made to stop her, but his phone rang again and, with a torrent of Italian words that she guessed she wouldn't find in the dictionary, he let her go.

It took twenty lengths of energetic swimming before Eden's temper dissipated, and she must have fallen asleep on the sun lounger, waking with a start to discover that it was six o'clock. Rafe's guests were arriving at seven, she remembered with a groan as she hurried up the steps of the villa. She needed to shower and do something with her hair. If she was going to be paraded in public as Rafe's mistress, she was determined, for the sake of her self-respect, to look as good as possible.

She flew across the marble hall, remembered she'd left her handbag in the sitting room and changed direction, coming to an abrupt halt just inside the door as four startled faces met her gaze.

'I'm so sorry.' Her cheeks flooded with colour and she edged backwards, vainly trying to hold her sarong in front of her to cover her tiny gold bikini.

Rafe had jumped to his feet while the other three men, Fabrizzio and two associates, stared at her expressionlessly. 'Eden, I thought you were upstairs, dressing for dinner.'

'Obviously not,' she quipped, trying to disguise her mortification with a smile. 'I must have fallen asleep by the pool.'

Fabrizzio Santini sat back in his chair and surveyed her clinically, as if she were a prize heifer in a cattle market. '*Buona sera*, Eden. Rafael mentioned you were staying at the villa for a while.' He paused fractionally and then murmured, 'I hope you are recovering well from your accident. I see you have been left terribly scarred.' The solicitude in his voice disguised the sting, but Eden felt it anyways and immediately tried to hide her injured leg behind the other one, lost her balance and would have fallen but for Rafe's biting grip as he caught hold of her arm.

Round one to you, Fabrizzio, she thought darkly, not taken in by his smile, and as soon as she had stepped through the door she shrugged free of Rafe's hold.

'What are you playing at? I thought you were getting ready,' he hissed, and she glared at him, her temper at boiling point.

'I told you. I fell asleep. I didn't get much last night, if you remember. There's still an hour until your guests arrive, apart from the early birds,' she added sarcastically. 'And was it really necessary for your father to mention my leg?'

'*Dio*, you are impossible sometimes. He was offering his sympathy, and no doubt trying to draw attention away from the fact that you were cavorting through the house half naked in front of the company's bankers,' said Rafe coldly. 'You'd better go and shower. And don't argue, you don't have time.'

Boiling him in oil would be too good for him, she thought bitterly half an hour later as she struggled with the zip of her dress. He was the most arrogant, annoying, chauvinistic male she'd ever met, and the tears that stung her eyes were from anger, not the loss of the closeness they'd shared in Venice.

To her amazement, dinner was not the ordeal she had dreaded. When she walked down the sweeping central staircase Rafe was waiting at the bottom for her and for a moment was unable to disguise the flare of hunger in his eyes as he took in her full-length, white halter-neck dress that displayed her curves and golden, tanned shoulders. Far from him wanting to hide her away, his voice rang with quiet pride when he introduced her to the array of business associates and their wives, and gradually Eden felt herself relax.

Fabrizzio was surprisingly courteous; indeed, it was he who insisted that everyone should speak in English rather than Italian, in deference to Eden, and Rafe felt his tension ease. Eden was wrong about his father. She'd obviously misunderstood his attitude towards her four years ago but she was older now and her new confidence meant she would be better equipped to deal with the strong-willed old man.

There had been no subterfuge between Fabrizzio and Gianni. No covert plan to rid her from his life. Gianni had lied; he had to accept that along with the fact that he would never know why. But his little brother had tried to make amends. He recalled a conversation between them months before Gianni had taken the overdose. In the throes of a deep depression, Gianni had suddenly taken great interest in his life and had questioned him on his future plans, what he would do when his racing days were over and the likelihood that he would marry and give Fabrizzio the grandchildren he longed for. Rafe had shrugged, his answer noncommittal, not daring to point out that Gianni had wrecked his relationship with the only woman who had ever been more to him than a brief diversion. Maybe his brother had understood more than he let on, he mused.

'Eden was always the girl you believed her to be.' Gianni's words still rang in his head, hardly an admission that he'd lied, but they had added weight to the decision he'd already made to find her, if only to bury the past and all its bitterness for good.

It was late when Rafe's guests departed, and Eden gave a

deep sigh of relief as she wandered into the sitting room and kicked her shoes off before collapsing onto the sofa. It had been a good evening, better than she'd hoped for, and she smiled as a slight movement from the terrace caught her attention.

'Rafe, what are you doing out there?'

'Rafael is taking a phone call in his office.' Fabrizzio Santini walked through the French doors and Eden's smile faded at the cold contempt in his eyes.

'I see,' she murmured quietly, and he gave a harsh laugh.

'I wonder if you do, Eden. Tell me, how long do you intend to act as my son's whore this time?'

'I don't need to listen to this.' Eden jumped up and headed for the door. Four years ago his patent dislike of her had unnerved her and she hadn't dared to stand up for herself, but a lot had changed since then. 'I don't know what you have against me, but out of respect for Rafe I think you should keep your feelings and your insults to yourself.'

She made to sweep past him but he gripped her wrist, so hard that she knew she would find bruises there later. 'I will not stand by and watch my son make a fool of himself over a cheap little nonentity,' he informed her in his gravelly, heavily accented voice. 'I thought I'd succeeded in getting rid of you four years ago, and I tell you now, Rafael will never marry you.'

Appealing to the swarthy Sicilian's softer side was a waste of time, Eden acknowledged. Fabrizzio wouldn't rest until he'd evicted her from Rafe's life once more and he was cunning enough to manipulate events in a way that wouldn't alert his son's suspicions. Attempting to convince Rafe of

Fabrizzio's hatred of her would be futile. Rafe adored and respected his father, the Santini blood ran thick and, although he had finally chosen to believe her over Gianni, his loyalties would be stretched to breaking point if she asked him to choose between her and Fabrizzio.

Fabrizzio's biggest fear, it seemed, was that Rafe would marry her. If only he knew how unlikely that was, she thought bleakly. There was no chance, and even less now that Fabrizzio had thrown down the gauntlet. Somehow she had to convince the older man that he had nothing to fear from her, that marriage to Rafe was the last thing she wanted. At least then he might leave them alone and wait for the affair to run its course.

'Actually, I have no intention of marrying your son,' she said coolly, and Fabrizzio gave her a disbelieving glare.

'I find it hard to believe that you don't want to get your claws into the Santini fortune.'

Eden shrugged. 'The price is too high. I don't want to live my life in a goldfish bowl, my every move reported in the tabloid Press. I'd be happy to settle for an English country house, a few acres of prime estate that I can cash in if necessary.'

Fabrizzio stared at her with his beady black eyes, as if he could see inside her head, and she shivered but held her ground, determined not to feel intimidated. 'And you think Rafael will buy you this house?'

'I'm working on it.'

'Perhaps I should warn my son that his English rose is a mercenary little bitch, available to the highest bidder.'

Nausea swept over her at his vile insinuations, but she lifted her head and met his gaze. 'Perhaps he already knows,' she suggested coolly. 'You have nothing to fear from me, Signor Santini. My relationship with your son is based on the most primitive of needs. To put it crudely, Rafe will slake his appetite and I will expect payment. I grew out of dewy-eyed romanticism a long time ago—four years ago, to be precise.'

Fabrizzio Santini had probably never been lost for words before, and Eden took pleasure in his momentary uncertainty. The expression on his face would be funny if she wasn't so close to tears.

'So for both of you it is a casual sexual liaison.' He assessed her with a speculative gleam in his eyes. 'Forgive me, but I'm not convinced. Four years ago you were in love with my son. What's changed?'

'I have, signor. I've grown up.'

She made her escape then before she broke down and spoilt the illusion that she had a heart of stone. A shower washed away her tears but it was harder to scrub Fabrizzio's contempt from her skin, and she wondered just what she'd done to make him despise her so much. The simple answer was that he was desperate for his remaining son to produce grandchildren with aristocratic Italian blood, and he'd seen her as a threat. Now that the threat, the fear that Rafe would choose her as his wife, was gone, perhaps he would leave them both alone.

There was no sign of Rafe when she slid into bed, and she guessed he was still working before they flew to Indianapolis for the next race of the season. She wished he would come to bed—she needed his solid strength and the reassurance of his touch—but eventually she fell asleep alone, and it was the early hours before he entered the bedroom to stare down at her with eyes that were as bleak as midwinter.

CHAPTER NINE

INDIANAPOLIS in August was hot and dusty. The car wasn't performing well; Rafe didn't make pole position on the grid, and, in an effort to lead the race, he pushed the engine too hard. Eden spent an agonising few minutes watching flames spew from the back of the car before he ground to a standstill, relief overwhelming her when she saw him climb out and stride away from the track.

'You're lucky you didn't burn to death,' she told him when they returned to the hotel. The heat and tension made her feel snappy and Rafe's unconcerned attitude didn't help.

'No one burns to death in Formula 1—the safety measures are stringent,' he said coolly as he headed for the shower. 'I'm more at risk of being nagged to death.'

'That's not fair.' Determined to keep his attention, Eden followed him into the *ensuite*. 'You have no idea what it feels like to watch a car go up in smoke, knowing you're still inside, although why I care beats me.' She glared at him, hands on her hips, her anger dissolving as she watched him shower. His body was to die for, she conceded, her eyes drawn to the way the soapsuds slid over the powerful muscles of his abdomen and then lower, down his thighs. She felt a familiar heat pool inside her and hastily dragged her gaze back to his face, mortification scalding her at the amused glint in his eyes. He knew exactly what she was thinking.

'Do you care, *cara*? I didn't realise.' That hateful, mocking tone that he used whenever he spoke to her lately was back, and she bit her lip.

'I know you're in a foul mood because you lost the race, but actually you've been pretty unpleasant since we left Italy,' she accused miserably. She didn't understand the reason for his sudden coolness towards her, but the closeness they'd shared in Venice had vanished and, although she'd asked him countless times, he simply shrugged and denied anything was wrong.

Persuading him to confide in her was like banging her head against a brick wall. He'd perfected stubbornness to a fine art and she was reduced to racking her brains for anything she might have done to upset him. All she could think of was the dinner party he'd hosted at the villa. His guests had been top executives from the business world, bankers, lawyers, and members of the highest echelons of Italian society. Had she inadvertently embarrassed him? she wondered. Admittedly, she'd felt nervous to begin with, but she hadn't made any major *faux pas*, like using the wrong fork or drinking from the finger bowl.

Perhaps the sight of her in her chain-store dress and costume jewellery had brought it home to him that she didn't fit in his world. She remembered how he had tried to persuade her to wear the pair of exquisite pearl and diamond drop earrings he'd presented her with.

'I'd be terrified of losing one,' she had argued as she ada-
mantly refused to try them on. 'If the sole reason you want
me to attend this dinner party is to display the signs of your
wealth then let's forget this relationship here and now.'

Being flaunted in public as his mistress was one thing, but
she was determined to hang on to her self-respect, and she
couldn't do that with speculation on just how she had earned
such expensive gifts.

'Are you ashamed of me?' she demanded huskily now, and
he frowned and reached for a towel.'

'Of course not. What a ridiculous thing to say,' he snapped.
'Why do you think I might be?'

'I don't wear haute couture or expensive jewellery like the
wives of the executives who attended the dinner party.'

'You could have done. It was your choice not to wear the
earrings I bought for you and you have several credit cards
at your disposal to buy clothes.'

'I know, but I prefer to pay for my own things. I've told
you I'm not interested in your money.'

'So you have,' he murmured, and she blinked at the barely
leashed fury behind the words. 'Your parsimony is admira-
ble, *cara*. Sometimes I wonder what you do hope to gain from
our liaison—apart from sex, that is.'

'That's a foul thing to say.' She had followed him through
to the bedroom and stopped dead, hurt beyond belief at the
deliberate cruelty in his tone. It was as if he was intention-
ally trying to upset her, and doubts formed thick and fast in
her head. Had he tired of her? Had she served her purpose
and he was pushing her away, preparing her for the end of
their affair? He hadn't made love to her since their trip to

Venice, and celibacy didn't agree with him, which could only mean one thing. 'Are you seeing someone else?'

'*Madre de Dio*, when would I have the time? You have an insatiable appetite, *cara*,' he murmured silkily, and she felt a tide of colour stain her cheeks. He made her sound like a nymphomaniac.

'Well, I'm sorry if I'm too much for you,' she said stiffly.

'Your eagerness to climb into my bed is flattering but sometimes I wonder if there's an ulterior motive behind it. Can you think of anything, Eden, anything you haven't told me?'

She shook her head in genuine confusion. 'You're talking in riddles, I don't know what you mean.'

He strolled across the room towards her and she couldn't drag her gaze from the minuscule towel around his hips that left little to the imagination.

'Perhaps it'll come to you,' he suggested blandly, 'and in the meantime I have no objection to satisfying your more primitive urges.'

There was something about this conversation that evoked vague memories, a hidden message in his mocking tone that she couldn't grasp.

'That's not a very nice thing to say,' she whispered, her eyes trapped by his dark, unfathomable gaze, and his slow smile sent ice slithering down her backbone.

'I don't feel very nice right now, *cara*.' His arm snaked out before she had time to react, his hand gripping her hair to yank her up against his chest. Droplets of water clung to his dark chest hair, heat and the exotic scent of the shower cream he had used assailing her senses, and to her abject shame she wanted to bury her face in him and breathe him in. 'Let's do something about those urges, shall we?' he breathed against her throat, but as she shook her head, murmuring a despairing protest, his fingers tightened in her hair.

'Don't even try to tell me you don't want this,' he hissed, his lips grazing her skin as he spoke. 'In this, at least, be honest, Eden. I watched you watching me in the shower and you're desperate, aren't you?' His mouth closed over hers in a kiss that warned of his absolute mastery, and pride demanded she resist, but her body had a will of its own and it was past caring about anything other than assuaging the driving need to feel him inside her.

He was breathing hard when he finally released her swollen lips, and his eyes travelled over her in a slow, assessing appraisal before he gripped the neckline of her dress and wrenched the material from her shoulders so that the buttons that fastened the front flew in all directions.

'Rafe! You didn't have to tear it.' His barely suppressed violence should have appalled her, yet to her shame she was filled with a fierce excitement. He would never hurt her, she knew that, but she recognised the urgency of his desire and it fanned the flames of her own.

'I'll buy you another,' he muttered as he dispensed with her bra, his eyes narrowing as he absorbed the rounded fullness of her breasts. 'Rest assured, I can afford you, *cara*.'

'I don't want your damned money,' Eden cried, desperately trying to cling to the edge of sanity while his hands cupped her breasts, and she drew a sharp breath as he lowered his head and lathered one nipple with his tongue before drawing it fully into his mouth.

'So you keep saying, which only leaves sex, because there's nothing else between us, is there?' His vicious taunts made her recoil and she tried frantically to pull away. In reply, he tugged a fistful of her hair until her back arched and he was able to torment her other breast, suckling hard so that she teetered on a fine line between pleasure and pain.

'Rafe, I don't want it to be like this,' she pleaded, 'not when you're angry and I don't even understand why.' He stiffened at her words but instead of releasing her, he scooped her into his arms and dropped her onto the bed. With one deft movement he stripped her of her knickers and pushed her legs apart with firm intent, before unwrapping the towel from his hips. He was all proud, arrogant male, fiercely aroused, and Eden closed her eyes in despair as the ache between her thighs throbbed unbearably.

'So stop me,' he challenged, his voice echoing the hardness in his eyes, and she swallowed.

'I can't,' she admitted on a sob of humiliation and misery at her own weakness, and he entered her with one powerful thrust.

Without the touch of his hands and mouth to arouse her, she was tight but no less ready for him and a groan was wrenched from him as her muscles closed around his shaft. He shouldn't have done that, shouldn't have taken possession of her so fiercely without any foreplay. Disgust at his own brutality made him attempt to withdraw, but she wrapped her long legs around him and held him fast.

'Don't stop,' she whispered, a husky sob leaving her when he continued to stare down at her, his body held still. 'What is it, Rafe—do you want to hear the words, do you want to hear me beg? All right,' she threw at him, her anger suddenly matching his, 'please don't stop, please make love to me…Rafe.' Her words were lost beneath his lips as with a muffled oath he initiated a kiss that drugged her senses, hot and passionate, demanding her response. She had no thought to deny him and kissed him back with a hunger that bordered on desperation, her body arching as he began to move within her, thrusting deeper and deeper, driving her to the edge, and she sobbed his name as he sent her hurtling over. He was right behind her, her name a savage imprecation torn from his throat as he slumped on top of her. But seconds later he rolled off the bed and marched into the *ensuite*, slamming the door behind him, and only then did she bury her head in the pillows, determined that he wouldn't hear her cry.

They had flown to Indianapolis on a chartered plane with the rest of the team rather than on his private jet, and on the journey home he avoided her, spending the time talking to the chief engineer. Eden was glad. They had nothing to say to one another, apart from goodbye, because he couldn't have demonstrated more clearly that their relationship was over.

As they were coming in to land he slid into the seat next to her and she instantly stiffened. He was invading her personal space and, worse still, the heat that emanated from his body and the clean, fresh scent of him made her want to bury her face against his chest.

'Are you all right?' he asked in a low, husky voice that even now did strange things to her insides. 'I behaved like an animal last night and I…' He hesitated and raked his hand through his hair. If he hadn't been so damned arrogant, she would have sworn he felt awkward. 'I should apologise.'

'Well, don't make a meal of it, I know how hard you find it to admit you're in the wrong.'

'I'm in the wrong?' He bristled with outraged pride, and heads turned at the sound of his raised voice. With a supreme effort he took a deep, calming breath and tried again. 'I'm trying to, how do you say, pour oil on the fire?'

'The expression is pour oil on troubled waters—pour oil onto a fire and it'll burn itself out, rather like our relationship, wouldn't you say?'

'We need to talk,' he muttered, and she gave a hollow laugh.

'We *needed* to talk,' she corrected. 'It's a bit late for that now. I don't know what terrible crime I've committed to make you so brutal, but I refuse to play mind games. You won't say what's bugging you, and after last night I really don't care any more.'

He visibly flinched at the word 'brutal,' his eyes dark and tortured, and she quickly looked away, fighting the compassion that was seeping through her. He'd always had a hot temper, her mind pointed out. He was a volatile Latin male and his mood swings were legendary, but although he hadn't hurt her physically last night, the mental wounds ran deep. She was his mistress, useful for only one thing, and she didn't think she could live that way for much longer.

At the airport they were whisked through Security but as they entered the main concourse she was blinded by flash bulbs as they were surrounded by a frenzied pack of Press reporters. It wasn't an unusual situation—Rafe was a national hero in Italy, and he only had to sneeze and it was headline news—but today the paparazzi's interest seemed to be focused on her.

Rafe hurled a stream of instructions to his bodyguards as he slung his arm around her shoulders and hauled her close, practically carrying her across the vast hall, but the reporters dogged them insistently, snapping at their heels like a pack of hyenas. This was a side of journalism she loathed, Eden thought as someone thrust a copy of that day's paper into her hands, and as she glanced at it the world tilted on its axis.

It would be hard to find a more unflattering photograph of her, she thought sickly as she studied the front page. It had been taken on the steps of the hotel in Indianapolis. Rafe looked every inch the playboy heartthrob in his dinner suit, and she was slightly behind him, hanging on to his arm and staring up at him with bleary eyes. She looked drunk, she noted disgustedly, although in fact she had been tired and miserable and had just tripped over a step.

Inside the front cover it got worse: pictures of her in her bikini that left little to the imagination and a horrific close-up of her scarred leg. But the photo that hurt most of all was the one taken in Venice. She was lying back in a gondola, seemingly smiling up at the camera, although in reality she'd been smiling at Rafe, and what had been one of the most romantic moments of their trip appeared tacky and distasteful. She looked like a hooker about to sell her wares.

'Oh, God!' she whispered, and Rafe snatched the paper out of her hands.

'Ignore it, it means nothing.'

'It means a lot to me—the pictures are *horrible*. I feel…*defiled*. I can't imagine how they got hold of them. It's as if someone was spying on us.'

'The paparazzi are everywhere,' he told her bluntly when

they finally reached the car and the chauffeur opened the door for them to bundle in. 'Their intrusion is just part of life.'

'Not my life,' she said quietly as she scanned the paper. She didn't speak much Italian but the written word was easier to follow and it was quite obvious that the article was a scurrilous, no-holds-barred account of their love life.

'Life in a goldfish bowl,' he murmured almost to himself, and she frowned, trying to remember where she'd heard the phrase before.

'They didn't get hold of this information by chance. Someone must have fed it to them, tipped them off about our trip to Venice. But who knew about it—only me and you?' She came to an abrupt halt, nausea churning in her stomach. For reasons she didn't understand he had been angry with her, but he wouldn't hurt her so cruelly, would he? 'Rafe, you didn't…?'

'*Madre de Dio!* That you could think even for one minute that I would do such a thing emphasises how little trust there is between us,' he said savagely.

'Then who, Rafe? Because someone has tried to humiliate me and they've damn well succeeded. Who else knew we were going to Venice?'

His father had known, whispered the insidious voice in Rafe's head, and he furiously blanked it. Not his father, no way. Fabrizzio might have disapproved of his relationship with Eden four years ago, but things were different now; he'd demonstrated that at the dinner party when he'd been so friendly towards her.

'Did you tell your father?' They arrived at the villa and she followed him up the front steps, her face a mask of misery that tugged at his heart even as he angrily refuted her suggestion.

'Leave my father out of this. Is it insecurity that makes you so jealous of my closeness to him, in the same way that you resented the bond I shared with Gianni?'

'No,' she denied furiously, 'but he doesn't like me. To him I'm just your whore. He told me that on the night of the dinner party,' she added shakily, quailing at the bitter contempt in Rafe's eyes.

'Was that during the conversation I overheard, in which you told him you were prepared to prostitute yourself for the sake of a house—I assume the Dower House?' he added silkily, and her legs buckled so that she collapsed in a heap on the marble floor of the hallway.

He made no move towards her, simply stared, his face a mask of arrogant indifference, and she bit back a sob. 'It wasn't what you think,' she whispered sadly. 'Fabrizzio's greatest fear is that you might choose to marry me rather than an upper-class Italian girl. I'm convinced he was behind Gianni's lies four years ago and I was certain he'd try to break us up again. I was trying to convince him that I'm not a threat.'

'You didn't need to go to such extraordinary lengths, *cara*,' he told her coldly. 'I could have told him that myself. You're the last woman on earth I'd choose for my wife.'

Eden sat at the kitchen table and cried until the tears ran dry and she was left with a pounding headache and red eyes. Rafe had disappeared into his office, the resounding slam of the door warning her she wouldn't be welcome, but she had no intention of trying to speak to him. It would be a waste of time. She didn't know exactly how much he had heard of her conversation with Fabrizzio, but obviously enough to condemn her without giving her the chance to explain how she really felt about him.

The bitter truth was that he wasn't interested and, even if she could find the evidence to prove Fabrizzio had been behind the Press tip-off, Rafe didn't want to know. He was a Santini and he would defend his family above all else. He adored his father and even now, when her heart was in pieces, she couldn't hurt him by forcing him to accept Fabrizzio's darker side.

'*Signorina.*' A tentative voice broke through her misery and she forced a watery smile as Sophia set down a cup of frothy cappuccino in front of her. She had established a firm friendship with Rafe's housekeeper but she was startled by the trace of tears on Sophia's cheeks. 'It is my fault,' Sophia sobbed, followed by a stream of Italian that Eden couldn't comprehend. 'The newspaper stories are so unkind and you are so upset, and it is my fault, I think,' Sophia managed to explain in her broken English.

'But how?' Eden queried gently. Sophia might have inadvertently revealed information about her life with Rafe to the media, but she would not have knowingly spoken to a reporter when she knew how much Rafe loathed the paparazzi.

'Signor Santini—we were talking, joking a little about how you were always too busy to eat the meals I prepared,' she confided with an embarrassed air. 'And he was interested to know when you were going to Venice.'

'Which Signor Santini?' Eden asked carefully. Rafe had

made the arrangements for the trip; he'd hardly have needed to discuss it with his housekeeper.

'Signor Fabrizzio,' Sophia whispered fearfully, glancing around the kitchen as she spoke, and Eden put a reassuring hand on her arm.

'Thank you for telling me. I promise you won't get into any trouble, Sophia.'

It only confirmed what she had already thought, she mused as she dragged herself upstairs and pulled her clothes out of the wardrobe. Fabrizzio had somehow been behind the newspaper article, but she would never convince Rafe of that. She spent the rest of the day alternating between misery and a growing anger that history was repeating itself. Fabrizzio had done his best to oust her from Rafe's life once before and she had let him do it without a fight, without defending herself. Against all the odds, Rafe had searched for her, he'd wanted to give their relationship another chance, and despite everything that had passed between them since she couldn't forget the closeness they'd shared in Venice.

He had been so tender, so *loving*, she recalled as a tiny flicker of hope burned in her chest once more. The exquisite attention he paid to making love to her and the softly spoken words he'd whispered in his native Italian were not the actions of a man who just wanted sex. Surely it had meant something special to him, as special as it had been to her, and she couldn't walk away from him again without one last attempt to bridge the chasm that had opened up between them.

As Eden took her place at the dinner table that evening, Sophia imparted the news that Rafe wouldn't be joining her. He'd left in a hurry an hour before, the housekeeper explained, and he'd given no indication of when he would be coming back. By midnight Eden had worked herself into a state of emotional meltdown, filled with a new determination to force Rafe to listen to her. His non-appearance stretched her already overwrought nerves and she paced the floor of the guest bedroom she had moved into, listening for the sound of his footsteps on the landing.

By one o'clock her imagination had clicked into overdrive as she pictured him with one of the gorgeous blondes who followed him avidly whenever he went out. He had to have found a bed somewhere, she reasoned, although it was debatable that he was sleeping in it. The thought of him making love to another woman made her feel physically sick and she hurried downstairs, wondering if he'd left a clue to his whereabouts in his study.

The sight of him sitting behind his desk knocked the air from her lungs as she stumbled to a halt in the doorway. But it was the haggard, almost shell-shocked expression on his face, and the emptiness in his black eyes, that made her gasp.

'Do you know what the time is? Where have you been?' Trepidation, mingled with relief that he was home, lent a sharp edge to her voice, and he stared at her, his eyes narrowing at the sight of her slender form.

'You sound like a nagging wife rather than an obedient mistress,' he murmured unpleasantly, and she flushed.

'Have you been drinking?'

He glanced at the half-empty bottle of whisky on his desk and poured a liberal amount into a glass before downing it in one gulp. 'I would say so, wouldn't you, *cara*?'

She should leave things until the morning, when they

might both be in a calmer frame of mind, but she'd been working herself up for a showdown all night and the temptation to fight her corner was too strong to deny.

'You have to listen to me,' she demanded, walking across the room to stand in front of his desk. 'I know it's not what you want to hear, but I can prove your father was behind the revolting articles in the papers. I know he set Gianni up to lie to you four years ago, and even persuaded him to kiss me in an effort to convince you to end our relationship.'

'He's obviously a busy man,' Rafe said with dangerous calm, and too late she recognised the burning fury in his eyes, her reactions too slow as he shot round the desk and gripped her shoulders. 'But not any more,' he continued, his temper barely constrained, and she winced as his fingers bit into her tender flesh as he shook her. 'My father suffered major heart failure late this afternoon. He's on a life-support machine and it's debatable whether he'll make it through the night.'

'Oh, God, I'm sorry.' She covered her trembling lips with her hand as the full horror of Rafe's words hit her. What if she had accused Fabrizzio unfairly? In her heart she knew she hadn't; he would have done anything to wreck her relationship with his son, and the clinical part of her brain noted that he'd even managed to suffer a heart attack at the right moment. Rafe would never listen to her now, and in all fairness she couldn't expect him to. All that mattered was that his father recovered, and, desperate to comfort him, she reached up and touched his face.

He recoiled as if she had struck him, and she shivered at the contempt in his eyes. 'Don't you dare offer meaningless words of sympathy when we both know how much you hate him. My father is dying and still you insist on trying to poison my mind against him,' he hissed, his teeth clenched as he sought to control his fury. 'But you're wasting your breath, Eden. I gave you the benefit of the doubt over Gianni—don't expect me to do it again.'

CHAPTER TEN

How could the sun still shine with its usual brilliance? Rafe thought as he stepped out onto the terrace. How could the bougainvillaea bloom with such fiery colour? His life was falling apart, yet the world looked on indifferently.

His parents' house had always been dark, but today it seemed like a mausoleum, and he was glad to escape its gloom, even though the sunshine affronted him. Children's voices, high-pitched with laughter, jarred the still air, followed by the hushed tones of their nanny as she tried to quell them. They were his cousin's two little boys—Marisa was in the house with his mother—and as he watched them playing he snatched a glimpse of the past. He saw two boys racing across the lawn on their bikes, each so determined to win that hurtling over the handlebars into the fishpond was a small price to pay for victory. He heard the booming laughter of the man who had urged them on, and the impish chuckles of his little brother.

'*Il Dio li benedice*—God bless you, Gianni,' he whispered huskily, past the boulder that had lodged in his throat. There was a curious pain in his gut—he felt as if he had been punched in the stomach—and his eyes were gritty and sore from the lack of sleep that was impossible while his father's life hung in the balance.

'Rafe!'

He tensed as a voice as cool and clear as a mountain stream slid over him, and for a moment he closed his eyes in despair. Eden! Wherever he turned she was there, quiet, gentle, bringing an air of calm to the huge, extended Santini family, who had gathered at his father's house to wait for news. Somehow, incredibly, since the night of Fabrizzio's heart attack a shaky truce had developed between them, down entirely to her steady insistence that she would not leave him while his father fought for life.

He wanted to shout and rave and tell her he didn't need her false pity, but, God help him, he needed her the way he needed oxygen to breathe and nothing, it seemed, could shake his intrinsic belief that she was the other half of his soul.

'The hospital just phoned with an update. No significant change,' she said softly, coming to stand beside him, and as he caught the drift of her perfume some of his tension drained away.

'You should go back to the villa,' he growled. 'It's a madhouse here.'

'I want to stay with you…I want to help.'

'I must go back in, my mother…'

'Is with the priest and her sisters. She wants you to go back to the villa for a few hours, Rafe. You need to eat and get some sleep.'

She was so beautiful, Rafe thought, so gentle in her compassion that his heart turned over. He had been unnecessarily cruel in Indianapolis, had behaved like a barbarian, and he closed his eyes, trying to shut out the knowledge that he must have hurt her, although even then she had been so responsive he ached at the memory.

'I need you.' The admission was wrenched from him. He was a strong man, proud and fearless—he had never needed anyone in his life until now—and Eden gave a low murmur, understanding his distress, as she wrapped her arms around him.

An hour later they returned to the Villa Mimosa to be greeted by Sophia's tear-stained face. Aware that Rafe had had enough, Eden took charge and steered Sophia to the kitchen with the request that she prepare something to tempt her master's appetite.

'I thought you'd agreed to a shower and a couple of hours' sleep?' she demanded as she caught Rafe heading for his study, where the phone rang constantly.

'There are people I need to speak to before the Monaco Grand Prix,' he argued.

'Petra has been your personal assistant for years, so she's perfectly capable of dealing with your calls, and you've been the head of the Santini group in all but name for months, ever since your father's first stroke. What's so important that you need to deal with it today?'

'Why do you care?' he asked huskily as he followed her up the stairs, and she stopped outside the master suite she no longer shared with him, staring at him with gentle compassion.

'I don't know,' she answered truthfully, remembering the hurt he'd inflicted. 'All I know is that I do.'

'I'll only go to bed if you come with me.'

The request shook her, the temptation to communicate in

the most basic, honest way tugging at her emotions, but she couldn't keep giving. He would drain her dry. 'You need to sleep,' she reminded him lightly, unable to hide the tremor in her voice. 'I'll come up and see you later.'

He slept for an hour and joined her for dinner, although he barely did justice to the meal Sophia had prepared before he returned to the hospital.

The next day followed a similar pattern until Eden received a phone call, Rafe's voice laced with pain as he explained that Fabrizzio had suffered another attack and was hanging on to life by the most tenuous of threads.

Eventually Eden went to bed. She had heard nothing more and dreaded the sound of the phone ringing, but sleep was vital if she was to be of any help to Rafe. She woke several hours later and fumbled for her watch to discover that it was three in the morning. Moonlight filtered through the shutters, slanting pale beams across the bed, and in its silver gleam she saw Rafe sitting, shoulders hunched, at the end of the mattress. The expression on his face, his silent agony, caused her heart to clench and her one thought was to comfort him as she moved to kneel behind him, sliding her arms around his neck.

'Is there any news on Fabrizzio's condition?' she asked fearfully, and he nodded.

'A slight improvement. He's from tough Sicilian stock and he won't give up his grip on life without a fight.' There was admiration in his voice, an affection he had never tried to hide, and she hoped with all her heart that, for his sake, Fabrizzio would make a full recovery.

'I'm glad,' she said simply, and he turned his head, his mouth searching for hers with an almost fevered desperation.

'I want to make love to you, *cara mia*. You have no idea how much I need the soft sweetness of your body right now.' His words were slurred with a mixture of exhaustion and pent-up emotions that were clamouring to be released, and she understood his need to find solace in the one place that provided sanctuary for both of them.

Perhaps it was a natural reaction, a reaffirmation of life, and she couldn't deny him when her own body was instantly on fire for him. He needed her and that was all that mattered.

He pulled her onto his lap and kissed her; long, slow kisses that drugged her senses and made her feel boneless and weak with longing.

'I hurt you in Indianapolis,' he muttered thickly against her throat. 'I was rough, brutal, and I am ashamed.' He lifted his head and she was shaken by the depth of emotion in his eyes, the self-loathing, and sought to reassure him.

'You didn't; I wanted you every bit as much as you wanted me. I think I rather proved that,' she added, her cheeks growing pink at the memory of her wild response to him.

'I'll be gentle this time,' he insisted as he scooped her up into his arms and strode into his bedroom. 'I have done things, said things to deliberately hurt you, yet you've shown me nothing but kindness while I pray for my father. Your compassion humbles me, *cara*. We need to talk.'

Eden reached up and laid her finger across his lips. 'Not now, Rafe; you once said that we communicate better without words and it's time to let our bodies speak.'

He shrugged out of his robe and untied the ribbons that fastened her silk negligee so that her breasts spilled into his hands while his lips found hers in a kiss that was full of ten-

derness, contrition and a plea for forgiveness. Passion overwhelmed her, stark and intense, desperate for fulfilment, and
she gasped as he moved lower to suckle her nipple with
gentle insistence until it was a hard, throbbing peak. When
he transferred his attention to the other she arched and dug
her nails into his shoulders as heat pooled between her thighs.

She wanted him now, her hunger white-hot, and she lifted
her hips in mute supplication, needing to feel him inside her.

'I won't rush it this time,' Rafe promised deeply. 'I will
make sure you are ready for me.'

'I am,' she muttered. She was in agony with wanting him
but he was determined to make amends for the last time,
when he had taken her with such selfish disregard for her
pleasure. Eden deliberately opened her legs and tilted her
hips, her heart thudding as she felt the rigid hardness of his
arousal against her thigh, but instead of entering her he caught
her two hands in one of his and lifted her arms above her
head.

'Patience,' he growled as he laved one throbbing peak and
then the other with his tongue while his hand slipped between
her legs and parted her, gently, delicately, before pushing
inside. His fingers explored her in an erotic dance and Eden
whimpered and tried to control the ripples of pleasure that
were building inexorably. She wanted to drag him up her
body so that he had no choice but to enter her, but her hands
were still pinioned behind her head and she twisted restlessly, almost sobbing his name as her climax neared its crescendo.

On the edge of ecstasy, he slipped his fingers out, the
weight of his chest a welcome burden as he drove into her,

slow, deep, filling her until she thought she would explode, and every thrust sent her higher and higher until restraint was smashed beneath the force of her contractions. Still he continued with his steady rhythm, although she was aware of the hoarseness of his breathing, his pace increasing, faster, deeper until he cried out her name and she clung to him while his body shuddered with the force of his release.

The aftermath was so sweet, she had never felt closer to him and knew she would never love anyone as much as she loved him. But did she have the courage to reveal how she felt, to tell him she had never stopped loving him throughout all the years apart, and was it really what he wanted to hear? She lay still, stroking his hair, and her heart missed a beat as she felt wetness against her neck, felt his shoulders heave as he finally gave in to the fear he felt for his father's life.

Over the next few days Fabrizzio stunned his doctors and family alike with the speed of his recovery. He still had a long way to go, but with his life no longer in imminent danger Rafe lost his look of haunted anxiety.

After the passionate night they had spent together, Eden had hoped their relationship would survive the traumas of the past few weeks, but Rafe seemed curiously reluctant to be alone with her. It was as if he regretted his display of emotion that night and hoped she hadn't read too much into it. He made no attempt to make love to her again or persuade her to move back into his bedroom, and her last vestige of pride meant that she refused to suggest it.

Pride made a lonely bedfellow, she conceded miserably after spending another night missing him so badly that she *ached*, not just for the pleasure he could give, but also for the feeling of oneness with the man who had captured her heart. He was polite and friendly but curiously distant, and in the run up to the Monaco Grand Prix she was forced to accept that they could never go back. Too much damage had been inflicted on a relationship that had been on shaky ground to start with.

On the day before they flew to the principality he received a visitor, a man she assumed to be a business associate, although Rafe never introduced her to him. After that his attitude towards her changed even more. He was excruciatingly polite and solicitous during the flight but the barrier he had erected between them seemed impossible to penetrate and she knew with a heavy heart that when the race was over it would be time to return to England to pick up the pieces of her life.

They arrived in Monaco to face a barrage of Press photographers as the world speculated on whether Fabrizzio Santini's close shave with death would affect his son's performance on the track. They needn't have worried, Eden thought bleakly as Rafe took the lead early on in the race and drove with a mixture of skill and sheer disregard for his safety. She only relaxed when he shot past the chequered flag, feeling as physically drained by nervous tension as if she had competed herself.

This was his life, she acknowledged as she watched him stand triumphant on the podium, spraying the crowd with champagne and grinning at the girls who flocked round him. He was a millionaire playboy with the world at his feet and, although she loved him more than life, she couldn't spend any more time chasing him round the world as his very public mistress, waiting for him to tire of her.

When they arrived back in Milan he escorted her over to the limousine but didn't slide in next to her.

'I'm going straight to the hospital,' he told her. 'Apparently Fabrizzio is sitting up in bed, demanding to take back control of the company.'

'Do you want me to come with you?' she asked, and he shook his head.

'Not this time; I want to see him alone. There are a few things we need to discuss,' he added, his expression suddenly grim. He didn't enlighten her further, but why would he? She wasn't part of his family, and now that Fabrizzio was recovering there was no need for her to hang around. His coolness towards her made that clear.

The villa was in darkness when Rafe's powerful sports car swung through the gates and roared up the driveway. No doubt Sophia would have retired to bed long ago, he thought grimly, a glance at his watch revealing that hours had passed since he had visited his father at the hospital.

What about Eden—would she have waited up for him? he wondered as he raced up the stairs. He should have phoned her but he'd been in shock, genuinely devastated by the conversation with Fabrizzio, and the only way he knew how to exorcise his demons was with speed. He must have covered hundreds of miles just racing up and down the motorways. Driving was second nature to him, the thing he did best, and while his attention was focused on the road he couldn't think about Eden and the way he had wronged her.

He didn't like guilt. It didn't sit comfortably on his shoulders, he conceded darkly as he pushed open the door of the guest bedroom that Eden had moved into. The bed was empty, stripped of its sheets, and a bolt of fear, greater even than when he'd heard of his father's heart attack, swept through him as he flung open the wardrobes and discovered they were bare. He had been preparing for the fact that she might decide to leave after he had spoken to her, after he'd revealed that he now knew the truth, but he hadn't expected to come home and find her gone.

Numbly he stumbled into the hall, his heart quickening as he saw the stream of light from beneath his bedroom door and he threw it open with such force that it creaked on its hinges. For a brief, joyous moment he thought she had moved back into the room they had once shared, but the suitcase lying open on the bed dashed his hopes.

'I wondered when you would turn up, or if you'd even bother,' she said coolly, carefully avoiding his gaze, but when he looked closely he noted the streaks of tears on her face and his heart turned over.

'Where did you think I'd gone, *cara*?' he asked gently, and she shrugged.

'I'm sure you have dozens of names in your phone book, you'd never be stuck for female company, Rafe.'

'The only company I want is yours,' he said forcefully.

'Oh, please! Let's not pretend that I'm anything other than a temporary diversion. I'm your mistress, nothing more, as you so clearly pointed out.'

'The night we arrived back from Indianapolis I was angry,' he began, but she shook her head wildly, and for the first time he noticed the perilous control she had over her emotions. She was practically breaking up before his eyes and he only had himself to blame.

'You were angry before, during and after Indianapolis,' she accused him furiously. 'I'm tired of always trying to pre-empt your moods, and nothing excuses your treatment of me. You blow hot and cold so fast I never know where I am with you,' she continued as weeks of hurt and frustration finally spilled over. 'While your father was ill I thought you actually needed me, but you don't need anyone, do you, Rafe? I provided a useful shoulder to cry on but since Fabrizzio has shown signs of recovery I'm no longer required. Your attitude towards me this last week is proof of that.'

It was proof that he had been left reeling from the information the private investigator had unearthed. He'd learned the day before they flew to Monaco that he had misjudged Eden so badly, he didn't stand a chance of winning her forgiveness. Not only that, but since he had demanded the truth from his father he now knew that he had misjudged her twice, the first time four years ago. The guilt he felt had been hard to handle; he didn't know how to approach her or where to start in begging for another chance, and his remorse had made him seem distant and aloof. Four years ago he had refused to listen to her, and he could hardly blame her for wanting to extract a bitter retribution.

'If you want proof of the way I feel about you, this is it,' he said calmly as he walked towards her, and she gasped as he pulled her into his arms and took her mouth in a devastating assault that left her trembling. 'This is all the proof we need,' he insisted when she stopped fighting and sagged weakly against his chest, but the tears in her eyes warned him the battle was far from won.

'The great sex was never in dispute,' she said quietly. 'But I want more than that, I deserve more. I don't want to be afraid to open a newspaper because there might be another picture or damning article about me. You didn't even defend my name, Rafe, you didn't care who was responsible for setting a photographer to spy on us in Venice. As your mistress I'm public property and I've decided to quit.'

'I know who set the paparazzi on us,' he told her urgently when she picked up her suitcase and headed for the door. 'And I have taken steps to ensure nothing like that will happen again. I would willingly protect you with my life, *cara mia*, and you will never suffer hurt like that again, I promise you.'

Eden studied him for several minutes, as if the blinkers had been removed and she was looking at him for the first time, and from her expression he guessed she didn't like what she saw. 'I don't believe you,' she replied with simple finality, 'and I want to go home.'

The sun was low in the late-September sky. It bathed the mellow stones of the Dower House in a golden glow and danced among the leaves that were beginning to turn russet in colour. She would miss the garden most, Eden thought as she wandered across the lawn and stepped through the French doors, before locking them for the last time. Nev would keep an eye on the house until the new owners moved in; he'd let slip that the sale had already gone through and, although he had assured her there was no rush for her to move out, it was time to go.

She watched the taxi turn into the drive with a sinking heart. Funny how she'd never really believed this day would come. She had clung to the pathetic daydream that Rafe would materialise and declare his undying love for her, but the reality was that he had spent the last month jetting around the globe in his bid for a sixth World Championship title. His decisive victory in Japan had sealed his place as one of the most successful Formula 1 drivers of all time and his picture had been on the front page of every newspaper, the obligatory blonde beauty at his side.

'Ready to go, love?' the taxi driver called cheerfully. 'I'll put your suitcase in the boot.'

'I'll just check I've locked the windows,' she murmured, furious with herself for giving in to the urge for one last look round. This had never been her home and it was ridiculous to feel so sentimental about it. It was a family house, a house that should be filled with children, but they wouldn't be hers and it was time to stop wishing for the moon.

She frowned when she came back downstairs to hear voices from the drive. Surely Nev would have told her if the new owners were arriving today? The bright red sports car caught her attention first—it was hard to miss—and her disbelieving gaze turned to find Rafe and the taxi driver practically coming to blows over her suitcase.

'Do you want me to stow it in the boot, or don't you?' the driver demanded belligerently.

'Yes!' Eden shouted as she stepped outside.

'No! Not yet,' Rafe qualified, and the driver let go of the handle in disgust.

'Well, when you've decided, perhaps you'll let me know,'

he snorted as he climbed into the car and turned the radio on. 'I'll just sit here and listen to the cricket while you make up your minds.'

'I've got a train to catch,' Eden warned, striving to sound cool and hide the fact that she was actually trembling. 'What do you want, Rafe?'

'Five minutes of your time,' he asked, with such serious intent in his eyes that she knew arguing with him would be pointless. 'I thought you loved this house,' he murmured as she led the way into the sitting room. 'I thought it was the reason you came back to me. That's what you told my father,' he reminded her, and she paled.

'You know why I said those things,' she whispered.

'To convince Fabrizzio that our relationship was a casual affair that meant nothing to either of us, rather than a prelude to marriage?'

'Yes.'

'Because you feared that if he saw you as a threat he would engineer a way of breaking us up, like he did four years ago? Only then, of course, he persuaded Gianni to help him,' Rafe said slowly, and she caught the note of pain in his voice.

'I honestly believe he did it because he thought it was best for you. He wanted you to marry an Italian heiress, not an English vicar's daughter with no social standing,' she replied hastily. Even now, after everything, she hated to see him hurt, and discovering that the father he idolised had betrayed him must be agonising.

'Actually the main reason he disapproved of my relation-ship with you was that he feared there was a high risk that any children we might have would be handicapped. He knew that your brother, Simon, was confined to a wheelchair, but not the reason for it,' Rafe added, his eyes never leaving her face. 'It doesn't excuse what he did, but it's an explanation of sorts.'

'Simon was hurt in an accident,' Eden said dazedly.

'I know and so does my father, now. He's also aware that, whatever the reason for Simon's condition, it would never have dissuaded me from wanting to marry you.'

'I see,' she murmured, still not really understanding why he was here. The real reason their relationship had foundered hadn't changed. He hadn't trusted her or believed in her and ultimately he didn't love her. Those things were a requisite of any relationship she embarked on from now on and she gave him a brisk smile, wishing that the sight of him didn't hurt so much. He was the sexiest man on the planet, she thought ruefully, but sadly she wasn't the only woman to find him so—the queue went twice around the block and she was tired of getting trampled on.

'I really have to go, so if that's all…'

'Of course it's not all.' The old Rafe exploded back on the scene, arrogant, demanding, his eyes flashing fire as he raked his hand through his hair and fought to contain his temper. 'I am trying to say I'm sorry,' he told her, faint outrage in his voice that she hadn't realised. 'I'm trying to make amends for the way I hurt you. Here,' he pulled an envelope from his jacket pocket and thrust it into her hands, 'this might explain things better.'

Eden stared at him and then slowly scanned the enclosed documents, her heart thudding in her chest as she carefully replaced them in the envelope and handed it back to him. 'It's a nice gesture,' she said huskily, her throat tight with suppressed tears, 'but no, thanks.'

'They are the deeds to the Dower House. I've bought it for you,' he yelled, as if raising his voice would make her understand.

'I know, and I can't accept it,' she replied with a calmness she didn't feel. 'You don't have to pay me off, Rafe, I came to you willingly, both times.'

'I'm not trying to pay you off. *Madre de Dio*, you are the most impossible woman I have ever met.' He glared at her, all powerful, dominant, angry male, and she tore her gaze from his mouth. She would not give in to the temptation to reach up and kiss him even though she yearned to with every fibre of her being. Loving him didn't mean it was right and his next sentence confirmed that.

'I haven't bought it for you alone—it's for us, for when I'm in England.'

It sounded worse and worse, he was planning to set her up as his resident mistress for when he happened to be passing through—a bit like a housekeeper with extracurricular duties, and the terrible thing was, she was tempted.

A glance at her watch revealed that time was getting on and she hoped the taxi driver wasn't charging her by the hour. 'I'm sorry, Rafe, but I'm not interested and if I miss my train I'll be late to check in at the airport.'

'I thought you were going to London. Your estate-agent friend told me you've got a job with a news agency,' he muttered as he followed her out of the front door.

'I have, but not in London.'

'So where—somewhere in Europe?'

'Sierra Leone,' she admitted. 'The news agency has asked me to write a series of special reports on the situation there.'

'Over my dead body, *cara*; it's too dangerous.'

'It will be over your dead body if you don't move out of the way of the taxi, and as for dangerous…' She broke off as words failed her. 'You're a racing driver, for heaven's sake! Don't talk to me about dangerous when I've stood at the trackside and watched you risk your life driving at ridiculous speeds for *entertainment.*'

'That's the other thing I came to tell you. I'm holding a Press conference tomorrow to announce my retirement from racing but I wanted you to be the first to know.'

He didn't know what he had expected her reaction to be—surprise, shock…he dared even hope for some indication that she was pleased, but instead she stared at him blankly as if he'd announced he was giving up eating chocolate. 'Well, I suppose you are getting on a bit,' she remarked finally, and the last vestiges of his patience went up in smoke.

'*Dio!* I can't do anything right. I buy the house you love and you throw it back in my face. I give up racing, the thing you hate most, and you act like you don't care.' He ran a shaky hand through his hair as Eden climbed into the waiting taxi. He needed some feedback here, some indication of her feelings, and adrenalin coursed through him as he tasted fear. This was the most important event in his life and losing wasn't an option.

'Tell me, *cara*, what do I have to do to make you come back to me?' He thrust his head through the open window of the car to glare at her, and Eden closed her eyes in despair. Another minute and she would be asking the driver to take her suitcase out of the boot again.

'You have to love me, like I love you,' she whispered, unable to hold back the tears as the car pulled away. 'It's all I ever wanted, Rafe, and the one thing you could never give me.'

She asked the man to drive away and was too busy scrubbing her eyes to take much notice of the passing scenery but the taxi driver suddenly braked sharply and muttered an oath.

'Road hog,' he shouted as he climbed out of the car. 'I recognise you now; you're that racing-driver bloke. Nice car,' he added with a sniff.

'Have it,' Rafe thrust the keys under the driver's nose as he slid behind the wheel of the taxi. 'I don't need it any more. I need a nice, safe, family car, isn't that right, *cara*?'

'I think you need to turn this car around and take me to the station,' Eden said shakily. 'What are you doing, Rafe?'

He made no reply but shot down the narrow country lanes so fast that she closed her eyes and when she opened them they were back outside the Dower House.

'Put me down,' she pleaded when he scooped her into his arms and carried her into the house. It was embarrassing enough that she had told him how she felt without him treating her like a rag doll, which was exactly how she felt right now.

'Of course I love you, you crazy woman,' he yelled, his temper at a simmering point as he headed for the stairs. 'My love for you was never in doubt.'

The look of stunned shock on her face told him she'd had plenty of doubts and still did, and his frustration disappeared, to be replaced with a rush of tenderness for the woman who was his very reason for living.

'*Ti amo, cara mia*. I see I'm going to have to work on your Italian,' he murmured gently. 'I've been telling you I love you for months, and in my dreams for years.'

Eden wriggled frantically in his arms, needing to escape him before she crumbled. 'You don't have to say it to make me feel better.'

'I'm saying it to make me feel better, *cara*. You are my life, my love and you have been since you fell through my hotel window and assured me that you were not a fan,' he told her softly and she swallowed at the depth of emotion evident in his dark eyes.

'But you didn't trust me, you believed I'd cheated on you with Gianni and you were so cruel. You broke my heart,' she accused huskily, and he lowered her to her feet, his arms around her holding her tight against his chest.

'If it's any consolation, I spent the next four years in purgatory. I missed you so much but Gianni had been horrifically injured and I couldn't leave him. It seemed wrong to search for happiness when he had none but I never forgot you, not for one day, and when I learned that you'd returned to Wellworth I knew I had to find you.'

'Have you really retired from racing?' Eden asked wonderingly. 'It's the most important thing in your life, Rafe, and I don't want you to make that kind of sacrifice for me.'

'You are my life, *cara*. Nothing else comes close. It's no sacrifice; I'm not giving up racing for you, but because I would rather be with you, in an English country house that we'll fill with our children.' His lips claimed hers in a kiss that touched her soul. Hungry, passionate yet filled with such tenderness that she knew with utter certainty that he was speaking the truth. Incredible as it seemed, this amazing, charismatic, infuriating man really loved her.

'Marry me?' he asked huskily as he trailed a line of kisses down her neck to the pulse that beat frantically at its base. She hesitated, the wariness back in her eyes. 'Your father…' she began, and he tilted her chin to stare down at her as if determined to blind her with his love.

'Knew that I wanted to marry you four years ago and that no other woman has ever come close. He also knows that his only chance of holding his grandchild is if I can persuade you to become my wife. Trust me, *cara*, he's hoping and praying you say yes.'

She had always loved this room, Eden thought as she glanced around the master bedroom that Rafe had used for the one night he'd spent at the Dower House. After he'd gone she had slept in his bed, desperate for some link with him, and she smiled as he laid her on the silk counterpane of the four-poster bed.

'Are you hoping I'll say yes?' she queried as he struggled with the buttons that fastened her blouse before impatience took over and he tugged so that the tiny pearls pinged across the room. He caught the remnants of uncertainty in her voice and sought to reassure her in the way he knew best, his lips caressing hers with tender passion until there was no room for doubt.

'Not hoping, *cara mia*, expecting,' he told her as his glorious arrogance bounced back. 'You are my other half, the keeper of my soul, and I love you with all my heart. You have to say yes because I will spend the rest of my life hounding you until you do and there are so many more pleasurable ways that we can spend our time.' He proceeded to demonstrate some of them and she linked her arms around his neck as he trailed his lips over her breasts.

'I won't waste time arguing, then,' she said breathlessly, lifting her hips obligingly so that he could dispense with her skirt. 'I love you, Rafe,' she whispered, and drowned in the emotion in his dark eyes as he made them one.

'And I love you, *cara mia*, always, for the rest of my life.'

BILLIONAIRES' BRIDES

Pregnant by their princes...

Take three incredibly wealthy European princes
and match them with three beautiful, spirited women.
Add large helpings of intense emotion and passionate
attraction. Result: three unexpected pregnancies—and
three possible princesses—if those princes have their way....

Coming in September:

THE GREEK PRINCE'S CHOSEN WIFE
by Sandra Marton

Ivy Madison is pregnant with Prince Damian's baby—
as a surrogate mother! Now Damian won't let Ivy go—after
all, he didn't have the pleasure of taking her to bed before....

Available in August:

THE ITALIAN PRINCE'S PREGNANT BRIDE

Coming in October:

THE SPANISH PRINCE'S VIRGIN BRIDE

www.eHarlequin.com   HP12660

REQUEST YOUR FREE BOOKS!

2 FREE NOVELS PLUS 2 FREE GIFTS!

YES! Please send me 2 FREE Harlequin Presents® novels and my 2 FREE gifts. After receiving them, if I don't wish to receive any more books, I can return the shipping statement marked "cancel." If I don't cancel, I will receive 6 brand-new novels every month and be billed just $3.80 per book in the U.S., or $4.47 per book in Canada, plus 25¢ shipping and handling per book and applicable taxes, if any*. That's a savings of close to 15% off the cover price! I understand that accepting the 2 free books and gifts places me under no obligation to buy anything. I can always return a shipment and cancel at any time. Even if I never buy another book from Harlequin, the two free books and gifts are mine to keep forever.

106 HDN EEXK   306 HDN EEXV

Name	(PLEASE PRINT)
Address	Apt. #
City State/Prov.	Zip/Postal Code

Signature (if under 18, a parent or guardian must sign)

Mail to the **Harlequin Reader Service®:**
IN U.S.A.: P.O. Box 1867, Buffalo, NY 14240-1867
IN CANADA: P.O. Box 609, Fort Erie, Ontario L2A 5X3

Not valid to current Harlequin Presents subscribers.

Want to try two free books from another line?
Call 1-800-873-8635 or visit www.morefreebooks.com.

* Terms and prices subject to change without notice. NY residents add applicable sales tax. Canadian residents will be charged applicable provincial taxes and GST. This offer is limited to one order per household. All orders subject to approval. Credit or debit balances in a customer's account(s) may be offset by any other outstanding balance owed by or to the customer. Please allow 4 to 6 weeks for delivery.

Your Privacy: Harlequin is committed to protecting your privacy. Our Privacy Policy is available online at www.eHarlequin.com or upon request from the Reader Service. From time to time we make our lists of customers available to reputable firms who may have a product or service of interest to you. If you would prefer we not share your name and address, please check here.

HP07